Anna Mei
Escape Artist

By Carol A. Grund

BOOKS & MEDIA
Boston

Library of Congress Cataloging-in-Publication Data
Grund, Carol A.
Anna Mei, escape artist / by Carol A. Grund.
p. cm.
Sequel to: Anna Mei, cartoon girl.
Summary: Anna Mei and her friend Danny have some difficult times over the summer when Anna Mei senses that Danny is hiding something from her.
ISBN 0-8198-0794-X (pbk.)
[1. Summer--Fiction. 2. Friendship--Fiction. 3. Family life--Michigan--Fiction. 4. Secrets--Fiction. 5. Chinese Americans--Fiction. 6. Michigan--Fiction.] I. Title.
PZ7.G9328Anr 2011
[Fic]--dc22
2010038172

Cover art by Wayne Alfano
Design by Mary Joseph Peterson, FSP

Published by Pauline Books & Media, 50 Saint Pauls Avenue, Boston, MA 02130-3491. www.pauline.org

Printed in the U.S.A.

AMEA VSAUSAPEOILL2-11J10-10157 0794-x

Pauline Books & Media is the publishing house of the Daughters of St. Paul, an international congregation of women religious serving the Church with the communications media.

1 2 3 4 5 6 7 8 9 14 13 12 11

Anna Mei, Escape Artist

This book is dedicated
to all the real-life
"Anna Mei"s and "Danny"s,
struggling to cope with the everyday
challenges of growing up.
My wish for you is that you learn to listen
to your own voice, and trust that there is
something wonderful out there waiting for you!

Special love and thanks to
Katelyn, Johanna, Melanie, Kristina, and Ana
—the bright and beautiful girls in my life
who helped inspire the Anna Mei stories.

Contents

Chapter One

Best Yearbook Ever

For possibly the first time in her life, Anna Mei Anderson was glad her last name started with an *A*.

A box filled with Elmwood Elementary School yearbooks had just been delivered to Room 117, and Ms. Wagner was planning to hand them out in alphabetical order. Anna Mei could hardly sit still—it would be the first time she'd seen one finished.

"But before I start," Ms. Wagner announced, "I want to recognize those of you who were on the yearbook staff—Michael, Elizabeth, Anna Mei, and Danny. Mr. Vogel told me how much he appreciated all of your hard work and leadership."

Anna Mei glanced over at the desk next to hers and found Danny—as usual—with his sketchbook open and a pencil in his hand.

"Pay attention," she whispered to him. "Ms. Wagner thinks you did something right for a change!"

He lifted his eyebrow in an innocent *who-me?* kind of way but kept right on drawing.

Ms. Wagner pulled a yearbook from the box and called out the first name on her homeroom list: "Anna Mei." She smiled as Anna Mei walked to the front of the room, a smile that reached all the way to her warm, blue eyes. "I'm so glad you joined our class this year," she said. "It's been a true pleasure getting to know you."

Anna Mei felt a rush of gratitude toward her homeroom teacher, one of the first people she'd met at Elmwood last fall. She'd been pretty terrified back then, standing in front of all those kids she didn't know. Ms. Wagner had been kind to her from the beginning.

"Thank you," she said, taking the yearbook and returning the smile. "I hope you'll sign it for me."

"I'd be happy to," Ms. Wagner agreed. "Be sure to bring it to the graduation party."

Before sliding into her seat, Anna Mei couldn't resist leaning over to see what Danny was working on. Unbelievable. In just those few minutes he'd managed to sketch two cartoon characters—a girl with straight, dark hair that just reached her shoulders, and a boy with freckles and a big grin. Both appeared to be hovering in the air, capes billowing out behind them.

Their arms were raised in a gesture of victory. Under the picture Danny had scrawled the words, *Yearbook Superheroes*.

Anna Mei had to look away quickly to keep from laughing out loud.

When she'd first come to Elmwood, she hated being the new kid. And she especially hated Danny Gallagher's sketches of her. She was sure that he was picking on her for some reason.

Eventually she figured out that Danny was really just a friendly guy who loves cartoons, food, and corny jokes, not necessarily in that order. Now she couldn't imagine school without him. In fact, she was the one who convinced him to join the yearbook staff with her, and now his playful sketches of life at Elmwood Elementary danced along the margins of almost every page. She and Danny may not be superheroes, exactly, but they sure made a pretty good team.

The new yearbook turned out to be the hot topic all day long, especially at lunch.

As usual, Anna Mei and Danny were sitting with Zandra Caine and Luis Hernandez. Danny once joked that their table would fit right in at the United Nations. During their heritage projects last fall, Zandra had talked about her African ancestors, while Luis's presentation was about Mexico. Anna

Mei, who'd been adopted by the Andersons as a baby, was born in China.

"Then there's me," Danny said, grinning, "the token Irishman."

Now Zandra was trying to flip through the yearbook with one hand while holding a sandwich in the other. "Really, I think it's the best one we've ever had," she said. "You guys did a great job."

Danny was already devouring the school lunch he'd bought—fish sticks with mac and cheese. "You're just saying that so we'll keep letting you sit with us," he said. "Which will definitely work, by the way. You may stay."

Zandra laughed. "That's so generous of you, Danny," she said, "considering we only have two days left in the whole year."

"Maybe he's already planning to rule the seventh grade lunch table, too," Luis suggested.

"Seventh grade!" Danny moaned. "Mind if I enjoy the summer a little bit before I have to think about that?"

"I know *I'm* going to," Zandra said. "And I'm really excited that you're coming to volleyball camp this year, Anna Mei. It's going to be a blast!"

"I can't wait," Anna Mei agreed. "I have so many ideas about what to do this summer that I decided to make a list."

"Only *you* would try to organize summer," Danny

told her with a big sigh, peeling the top off his container of applesauce.

But before Anna Mei could come up with a good comeback, Zandra suddenly stopped turning pages and said, "Hey, look at this!"

The three others crowded in closer to see.

Zandra was pointing at part of a collage with the title "Fall Follies" at the top. The picture was pretty small and a little blurry, but it was still easy to recognize the four girls standing in the gym, all dressed as cowgirls: Zoey, Rachel, Amber, and—

"Anna Mei!" Danny yelled.

Chapter Two

What's Wrong with This Picture?

For a moment it seemed as if all the other noise in the cafeteria had stopped, so that everyone could concentrate on staring at them.

"Wow, Danny—dial it down a notch, will you?" Luis said, running a hand through his thick, dark hair and looking nervously around the room.

"Sorry," Danny said, lowering his voice to human level again. "It's just that I can't believe you let them put that picture in there, Anna Mei."

She swallowed hard, trying to push down the queasy feeling that had started creeping up from her stomach. *Let them put it in?* She hadn't worked on that page. And she'd never seen that picture before in her life.

Zoey, Rachel, and Amber had been her first

friends at Elmwood. Well, okay, maybe not exactly her *friends*, but they had at least made an effort by inviting her to join their club. At first, Anna Mei had been grateful—and relieved. Being in the Ponytail Club had meant she had someone to sit with at lunch, someone to talk to between classes.

Of course, it had also meant pretending to be just like them—girls who loved horses, thought school was boring, and believed kids like Danny belonged on another planet. At first Anna Mei thought that lying and pretending were worth it. Any friends were better than none at all, right?

But the whole situation had spiraled out of control pretty fast. One day she was Anna Mei, newly transplanted from Boston and a little unsure of how this new school thing was going to work out, and the next she was someone she barely recognized.

It turned out that the new personality she'd tried on didn't fit any better than the oversized cowboy boots she was wearing in that yearbook picture. She'd borrowed them from Amber to wear to the Follies. But clomping around in them that night had been a real low point, which she'd managed to make even worse by hurting the feelings of the one person who had wanted to be her friend all along—Danny Gallagher.

Luckily, he had stuck around anyway. And he turned out to be the one who helped her find her way back to the real Anna Mei. She'd never imagined that the answer to a prayer could be a red-headed, freckle-faced, cartoon-loving boy—but that's how things had worked out.

Now she looked across the cafeteria to the table where Zoey sat, her long ponytail trailing down her back as she paged through her own yearbook. Amber sat beside her, and Rachel across from them. The seat across from Rachel, the one where Anna Mei used to sit, was empty. Anna Mei could just imagine the conversation—probably something about how lame the yearbook was and how Danny's drawings had ruined the whole thing.

She took a deep breath. The queasy feeling had gone back where it came from.

"Give me a break," she said, then reached out and snapped the yearbook shut. "I was new here, remember?"

Zandra stood up and put her arm around Anna Mei's shoulders. "We know," she said. "That was a long time ago."

"Yeah, don't sweat it, Cartoon Girl," Danny said. Anna Mei hadn't liked that nickname at first, but it didn't bother her anymore. Besides, her name really did sound like *anime*, those Japanese cartoons he was so crazy about. "It took a little time for me to grow on you, that's all."

The other three looked at each other, grinning. "Just like mold!" they all said at the same time.

When the dismissal bell rang at three o'clock, Anna Mei took her time zipping up her backpack, waiting while the other kids streamed out the door. They'd spent the last few days helping Ms. Wagner clean the room. Now with all the shelves and bulletin boards empty, and the science equipment packed away, Room 117 looked like it had already left for summer vacation. Seeing it like that made Anna Mei realize that even though she hadn't been here very long, her days at Elmwood Elementary were really coming to an end.

"Feeling nostalgic already?" Danny asked from the doorway, where he stood waiting for her. "Maybe Ms. Wagner will let you come back and clean test tubes once in a while."

She sighed. "I guess I'm a little sensitive, but it feels like I just changed schools, and now I have to do it all over again."

"At least we're all going to Westside together," he told her.

"That's true," she agreed, as they headed down the hall toward the front doors. "And the party on Friday will be a lot of fun. I can't wait to finally meet your parents and Connor. Are you guys doing anything special first?"

He shook his head. "My dad can't get off work early enough for that. We'll have just enough time to make it to the ceremony as it is. And I wouldn't count on Connor being there—now that he can drive, he's hardly ever around anymore."

They stepped outside where the buses were lined up at the curb, loading quickly. They would need to hurry to catch theirs.

"Then come with us," Anna Mei said. "My aunt and uncle are getting a babysitter and meeting us for dinner at Delaney's. We can pick you up on the way."

Danny looked doubtful. "I don't know if—"

"Come on," she said, cutting him off. "You know they have great food there. And you won't have to worry about being late for the ceremony."

He stopped at the open door of his bus. "Are you sure your parents won't mind?" he asked.

"Oh, right," she said, laughing. "Like they won't have twice as much fun with you there."

It was true—her parents always liked having Danny around. After all, her father's sense of humor was pretty much stuck at the level of a twelve-year-old boy's anyway.

"I'll tell them it's all set!" she called out as he disappeared up the steps.

The door closed, swallowing Danny inside the bus. As it started to pull away, she expected him to yell back or make a face at her from the window. But in her last glimpse of him, he was slumped down in a seat near the back, not looking at her at all.

Chapter Three

A Changing Room

After dinner that night, Anna Mei's father volunteered to do the dishes on his own so she and her mother could go upstairs and pick out an outfit for the graduation ceremony.

Now that they'd gotten rid of the hideous wallpaper and carpet that had been here when they moved in, Anna Mei's room was her favorite part of the house. She had ignored the Ponytail girls' advice about painting the walls lime green, sticking instead with her favorite shade, *Parfait Pink*. But since her father had already bought the green paint, she'd decided to try putting it on the trim and furniture, even the closet doors.

It turned out that those two colors looked fantastic together. Even on the cloudiest days her room seemed bright and cheerful. When Lauren, her best friend from Boston, had visited at Christmastime, she'd raved about how pretty it looked. "I can't believe this is the same room as the one in the pictures you sent me," she'd said.

Mom sat down in a green and white striped chair next to the window. She had already looked at Anna Mei's yearbook but now turned the pages slowly, examining each one as carefully as if it might contain clues to a hidden treasure.

"I just can't get over what a great job you kids did on this," she said.

"Mom, you've said that, like, ten billion times already," Anna Mei pointed out.

"All I know is that I worked on my high school yearbook, and it wasn't nearly as professional looking as this," Mom said. "And no jokes about the dinosaur age, young lady."

Anna Mei smirked. That *did* sound like something she would say. She opened the closet door and started taking out the new clothes they had bought a few weeks ago, after realizing she'd outgrown pretty much everything from last summer.

"Well, everything is digital now," she said. "We used a lot of special software."

Anna Mei's grey and white cat jumped into Mom's lap. With Anna Mei unavailable at the moment, Cleo must have decided that any lap was better than none.

"That may be true, but no computer wrote the stories, or the captions," Mom said, holding the yearbook with one hand and petting Cleo with the other. "And Danny's drawings are really charming. Are you going to have your friends sign it?"

Anna Mei laid her clothes on the bed. "We're supposed to sign them at the party on Friday," she said. "Most of the kids have been going to Elmwood since kindergarten, so they're going to want a *lot* of signatures."

"You know, I've been thinking about that," Mom said. "It must feel kind of strange for you, to be graduating from sixth grade here. If we'd stayed in Boston, you would just be finishing your first year of middle school now."

"Well, yeah," Anna Mei answered, going back to the closet to look for shoes. "Of course it feels strange. I thought we'd live there forever, and that I'd always have the same friends, and we'd all graduate from high school together."

But when she turned and saw the look on her mother's face, she instantly wished she could take the words back. She didn't want Mom to feel badly about her decision to move the family here last fall—those days were over.

She sank down on the bed, needing to think, wanting to choose just the right words this time. For a moment, Cleo's purring was the only sound in the room. But when Anna Mei was ready, her voice came out clear and strong.

"You know I didn't want to move here," she said, "and I had a really hard time at first. But when you think about it, I didn't start out in Boston, either."

"I guess that's true," Mom said.

"You always told me that you and Dad went to China to adopt me because I was meant to be your daughter—that it was God's plan. So I figure this is part of the plan, too, and I just have to trust that I'm where I'm supposed to be."

Mom sighed, shaking her head. "Excuse me," she said, "but exactly when did you get so wise?"

Anna Mei smiled. "Well, I am practically a sixth grade graduate, you know."

"As if I could forget that," Mom said, with a wistful *my-little-girl-is-growing-up* kind of sigh. Anna Mei figured she'd better get the conversation back on track.

"So, which one do you like best?" she asked, waving an arm toward the clothes on the bed.

"Hmmmm. I think I'd vote for the lilac skirt with the white cardigan."

Anna Mei took those over to the mirror and held them up. "These are nice," she agreed, "but I'm leaning toward the black and red dress. It's a little more . . ."

"Colorful?"

"I was going to say *sophisticated*, but I didn't want you to freak out or anything."

Mom laughed. "This from a girl whose idea of high fashion used to be polka dot high-tops and T-shirts with sparkles."

"Come on, Mom, I was like, six years old then."

"Well, it seems like yesterday to me," she said, clearly in danger of doing that sighing thing again.

But instead she stood up, deposited a protesting Cleo back in the chair, and came over to put her arm around Anna Mei. "You're going to look beautiful in whatever you pick. And your dad and I will be so proud of you."

"Thanks, Mom. I'm glad Aunt Karen and Uncle Jeff are coming, too."

"Me too," Mom said. "Which reminds me—does Danny know our reservation is at five-thirty?"

"Yeah, I told him we'd pick him up a little after five. I knew you guys wouldn't mind."

"Of course not," Mom said. "You know he's always welcome. I just wish his parents were able to come. I have a feeling that your dad and Mr. Gallagher would get along like a house afire, as your grandfather used to say."

"Okay, that's just weird," Anna Mei said, laughing. "I don't even want to know what it's supposed to mean. But I guess we'll find out if you're right when they meet at the party."

Mom picked up the black dress and handed it to Anna Mei. "Then let's get the fashion show started. As you can see from my own attire," she said, gesturing to the dark blue nursing scrubs she was still wearing from work, "I could use a few tips on sophistication myself."

Chapter Four

Missing

Snaking slowly through the gym, a double line of sixth graders processed past rows of seats filled with parents, siblings, and teachers. A recording blared out the *dum, dah-dah-dah-daaah-dum* music that Ms. Wagner had called "Pomp and Circumstance" at rehearsal this morning, but which they all just thought of as the "Graduation Song."

Anna Mei had to smile, and not only because of the millions of cameras and camcorders going off all around her. She just thought it was funny that the teachers had decided to line them up for the procession by height instead of alphabetically. Which had put Anna Mei . . . right in front anyway.

They joked about it at dinner. "Doomed to always be first," Danny teased her. "You might as well get used to it."

"You're laughing now," she shot back, "but just wait until I'm the first person to land on Mars."

Aunt Karen reached over to high-five her. "You go for it, Anna Mei," she said. "I'd bet all my money on you!"

"I would, too," Uncle Jeff agreed. "If we had any, that is."

"Well, I'm pretty sure NASA has a height requirement," Dad said, sounding worried but aiming a wink in Danny's direction. "If I were you, Anna Mei, I'd get busy inventing some platform astronaut boots over the summer."

The server arrived with their food then and Anna Mei found herself blinking back a sudden mistiness in her eyes. She loved having her family all together, laughing and joking, and celebrating with her. And having Danny with them made it that much better.

She smiled and thanked them as they raised their glasses in a toast. Then she added a silent prayer of gratitude for everything that had brought her to this moment.

During the graduation ceremony, Anna Mei discovered that being at the front of the line actually had its perks. Once she'd gone up to get her certificate from the principal, she could just relax and enjoy watching everyone else. Danny pretended to trip over her feet on the way up. Zandra laughed out loud when one of her brothers yelled, "Go, Zannie!" during her turn.

But there was a moment, during a speech by a classmate Anna Mei didn't know very well, when she felt a twinge of sadness for what she'd left behind. "We've spent so many years together," the girl said, "most of us starting in kindergarten. We've built so many friendships and made so many memories."

It made Anna Mei think of her own long-time classmates, who were probably together somewhere back in Boston, laughing and making plans for a summer that didn't include her. She'd never forget them. She hoped they would think of her sometimes, too.

Dum, dah-dah-dah-daaah-dum! The music started again. She wasn't a sixth-grader any more, and it was time to move on.

At the party afterward, Anna Mei left her parents chatting with Zandra's. She figured their conversation would be mainly on the theme of *can-you-believe-we're-old-enough-to-have-kids-in-junior-high-already?*, and she didn't need to hang around for *that*.

Searching for Danny in the crowd, she stopped to sign what seemed like a hundred yearbooks. Ms. Wagner wrote a special note on the Room 117 page, and Mr. Vogel thanked her again for all her work. Mrs. Marshall, the secretary who had escorted Anna Mei through the school on her very first day, came up and gave her a big hug.

But no Danny. She did run into Luis, who said he hadn't seen Danny since the ceremony. "Did you check the refreshment table?" he asked.

She had—twice. Both times she'd expected to see him standing there, a cookie in each hand. Where could he be?

Finally she made her way back to her parents. "I don't understand it," she told them. "Danny and his parents must be here someplace, but I can't find them."

"They *were* here," Dad said. "Danny came by about a half hour ago and told us his mother wasn't feeling well, so they were going home early. He said he'd talk to you tomorrow."

Disappointment stabbed at her, making her feel like a balloon with the helium leaking out. "I can't believe they left already," she said. "I didn't even get to meet them."

"Maybe they could come over for dinner sometime," Mom suggested.

"I guess so," Anna Mei said. "That would be fun."

But even as she said it, a nagging little thought wriggled its way into her brain and settled there—a thought that somehow, that dinner was never going to happen.

Chapter Five

Organizing Summer

"So you really did make a list," Danny said, helping himself to a handful of pretzels.

They were stretched out on lounge chairs in Anna Mei's backyard, shaded by one of the giant elm trees that dotted the lawn. She had brought supplies from the house—juice, pretzels, and her favorite notebook, the one with planets and stars on the cover.

"This list is going to keep us from wasting the whole summer doing nothing," she told him, flipping the notebook open to the right page.

"Huh," he answered, sounding less than enthusiastic. "You realize that for most people, that's exactly the point of summer."

"Well, it's my first summer here," Anna Mei pointed out. "I don't want to miss anything."

"Like what? This isn't exactly the middle of New York City."

"That doesn't mean there's nothing to do," she insisted. "I've been jotting down some ideas, and I thought you might have some."

She poured them each a glass of juice, then settled back to drink hers while he read what she'd written:

Things To Do This Summer

Visit nature center
(observe plant/animal species)
Science museums/exhibits
(Ann Arbor, Kalamazoo)
Planetarium (learn constellations)
Read "Outward Odyssey" series
Tennis? Swimming? (Find out where)
Volleyball camp

"So what do you think?" she asked.

"Some of it sounds okay," he said, "but there are too many words like 'learn' and 'observe' in it."

"Well, those are just science terms," she pointed out. "You can't go wrong with science."

"Something I would probably debate if we were in school, but the point is . . ." he looked over at her, paused, then finished dramatically, "we're *not*."

She had to laugh then. That was pretty hard to argue with, after all. The hot sun, the bright flowers around the patio, the distant hum of a lawnmower—the whole day practically shouted summer, with a capital S.

"I get your point," she said, "but admit it—everything on here will be fun. We can ride our bikes to the nature center. My dad already promised to take us to the science museum in Ann Arbor. And there's a planetarium right near here, at the university."

"Yeah, I've been there a couple of times," Danny said.

Anna Mei's father, a research scientist, had started working at the university when they'd moved here last fall. But Danny's father had worked there for years, in the maintenance department. Of course, for how many years she had no idea. Lately she'd begun to realize how little Danny actually said about his family.

He certainly hadn't wanted to talk about what happened with them at the graduation party last week.

"She's feeling better. Just a little tired," was all he had said when Anna Mei asked about his mother. "So did anything exciting happen after I left? Any teachers decide to retire rather than face life at Elmwood without me?"

She had planned to tell him how flat the party had seemed without him, and how disappointed she felt about not meeting his parents after all. But he brushed the whole thing aside so quickly that making a big deal about it suddenly seemed awkward.

"Did your dad take you to the planetarium?" she asked now.

He frowned, looking as if he was trying to remember. "I think so, back when I was little. But I've been there on school trips a couple of times. It's pretty cool, actually. I'm sure a star freak like you will love it."

"And *I'm* sure you mean that as a compliment," she said, grinning. "So we'll keep planetarium on the list. Don't you have any ideas to add?"

"Just one," he said. He took the pencil from her, wrote something on the list, then turned the notebook around so she could see it.

Anna Mei sighed. *Of course*. The word he'd written was "anime." Ever since she'd known Danny, he'd been trying to convince her that Japanese cartoons were the greatest source of entertainment ever created. He loaned her books about anime and manga, and brought over DVDs he called "classic."

"Okay, I'll compromise," she said. "We'll just say 'movie nights,' and I get to pick some of the movies."

"Deal," he agreed, fishing out the last few pretzels from the bag. "As long as enough popcorn is involved, I can watch anything."

They both looked up at the sound of Anna Mei's mother opening the sliding glass door and stepping onto the patio.

"I should take a picture of you two sitting out

here," she said, coming across the grass to join them. "You could call it, *What I Did on Summer Vacation*."

"Don't get too used to it, Mrs. A.," Danny told her. "This may be the last time you ever see us relaxing."

"Oh? Did you secretly enroll in summer school?"

Danny handed her the notebook, still opened to Anna Mei's list. "She's trying to plan practically every minute. And you'll notice there's nothing on there about sleeping in or goofing off."

Anna Mei shrugged. "Since I'm sure you'll be goofing off no matter what we do," she said, "I didn't bother to write it down."

"I don't know, Danny. All this stuff looks pretty fun to me," Mom said, and Anna Mei shot him a look that meant *I told you so*. "I'm hoping you'll be able to include a family vacation on here, Anna Mei. If Dad and I can both get time off, we want to visit Boston in August."

"That would be great!" Anna Mei said. It would be their first time back since the move. And she could think of about a *million* things to do in Boston, especially with Lauren.

"And make sure you leave room on your schedule for girl time," Mom told her. "I've been making my own list of places for us to check out around here."

Every summer since Anna Mei could remember, she and her mother had spent leisurely mornings sharing pancakes at a local restaurant, followed up by trips to the bookstore or the mall.

"I think I can squeeze you in," she said, smiling. "Just call my office for an appointment first."

"Right now I have an appointment with some thirsty flowers," Mom said, handing the notebook back to Anna Mei. "It's starting to get hot out here already."

Back at the patio, she attached a spray nozzle to the garden hose, then turned on the water. They watched as she watered all the flowers growing in pots and baskets around the patio, the cool, clear spray catching the afternoon sun and making the bright petals sparkle.

When she'd finished and gone back into the house, Danny yawned and stretched. They'd been out here long enough for the sun to move high overhead, turning their patch of shade to a bare sliver. "It *is* kind of hot out here," he said. "Maybe we should go inside and play video games or something."

Anna Mei frowned. "That's not a very interesting way to spend our first day."

"And I suppose you have a better idea?"

"Well . . ."

She poured herself the last bit of juice, hoping to kill some time while she tried to think of an answer. When she lifted the glass, she glanced toward the patio and noticed some water still dripping from the hanging baskets. That's when inspiration hit.

"As a matter of fact," she said, "I do."

She stood up slowly and took a tentative step toward the patio.

"What?" Danny asked, following her gaze. It only took him a couple of seconds to figure it out.

"Oh, no you don't!" he exclaimed, and in the next instant they were running across the yard at top speed, laughing and yelling, both trying to be the first one to reach the hose.

Chapter Six

Maybe Next Time

Anna Mei was lying on her back, looking up at a sky as blue as the wildflowers waving in the meadow all around her. She could smell their sweet fragrance, which somehow seemed to mingle with the scent of freshly mown grass, although there didn't seem to be any grass around. She didn't see any trees either, yet birdsong filled the air.

Suddenly one sound began to drown out the others—a *tap tap tap* that must mean a woodpecker was nearby, knocking its beak against the tree bark over and over. Then another bird let out a loud, wailing cry: "Anna Mei? Anna Mei!"

Anna Mei opened her eyes and the meadow dissolved as if made of mist. Her bedroom was full of sunlight, and the window was open, letting in both a soft breeze and the sound of birds chirping. Her mother stood at the door, knocking on it and calling her name.

"I was about to come in there and take your pulse," Mom said. "You've turned sleeping into an art form lately."

"I guess I stayed up a little too late reading," Anna Mei said, yawning. The usual warm lump that kept her from stretching her legs out seemed to be missing from the end of her bed. "Where's Cleo?"

"I fed her an hour ago," Mom said. "She must have thought you were a lost cause. But you need to get going now or we're going to run out of time."

Anna Mei's head still felt a little groggy. "Time for . . . ?"

"It's Friday," Mom said, coming over to sit on the edge of the bed. "We're supposed to go out for breakfast, remember? Although now I guess it will be more like brunch. I have to be at work at noon."

Anna Mei sighed. Rushing around and getting ready to go out was the last thing she felt like doing. "Can't we go another time?" she asked. "Dad's taking Danny and me to the science center tomorrow, so I'd like to take it easy today."

"Well, it's not as if I'm asking you to spend the day at hard labor. It's just breakfast."

"You know what I mean," Anna Mei said. "I'm not really hungry yet, anyway. I'll just fix myself something later."

Mom hesitated a moment, then said, "All right, but let's make it soon, okay? I miss seeing you when I work these long shifts."

When her mother had gone, Anna Mei propped her pillow up behind her, grabbed her book from the nightstand, and started to read where she'd left off.

"You guys have *got* to see this!"

Anna Mei had left Danny and her father tinkering with the machines and mechanical toys inside one of the Ann Arbor Science Museum galleries. After going off to explore on her own, she came back to tell them about an amazing exhibit she'd discovered.

Danny looked up from the weights and pulleys he was using to build a giant block tower. "Are they about to close it down or something?" he asked.

"No, I just can't wait to show it to you."

"Well, *I'm* certainly intrigued," Dad said. "You weren't even this excited about the rock wall."

Climbing the rock wall *had* been fun—in fact, they'd been having a great time ever since they'd arrived at the museum this morning.

Up to now her favorite part had been the nature room, where they'd seen dozens of caterpillars feeding on apple leaves and spinning cocoons. While they stood at the observation window, a Monarch butterfly had poked free of its dark chrysalis. It crawled through a crack along the bottom, then clung to the chrysalis upside down, slowly flapping its orange and black wings. At first they were tiny, all crumpled and damp, but the exhibit sign explained how the flapping was actually pumping liquid into the wings' veins. In only an hour, the butterfly would be able to fly on its own.

"That's so cool!" Danny said, standing beside her.

"That's *metamorphosis*," she said. "I've never seen it happen live before."

"Oh, I've seen it plenty of times," her father told them. "And you know what I always say about it, right?"

Anna Mei knew better than to ask, but Danny took the bait. "No, what?"

"That I never metamorphosis I didn't like!"

Danny laughed, naturally. He'd been over at their house a lot in the two weeks since graduation, but he never seemed to get tired of hearing Dad's corny jokes. And Dad seemed to love having such an appreciative audience. Anna Mei was glad they got along so well, even if she sometimes felt like the adult shaking her head at the kids.

"Okay, let's see this incredible exhibit of yours," Danny said now, giving up his spot with the pulleys. "But it better be good."

Anna Mei led them down the hall and into a small, dark room labeled ViewSpace. Soft music played from speakers in the ceiling as the three of them sat down in front of a large screen. At first the picture projected there looked like a beautiful still shot of constellations in deep space. But as they watched for a minute, the image moved, becoming a kaleidoscope of changing light, color, and shadow.

"Wait, is that a live shot?" Dad asked. "From space?"

"Exactly," Anna Mei said. "The Hubble Space Telescope is filming it, then sending the images over the Internet. The shots were taken from *above* those stars. They broadcast live images like these all day long, but they also show mission updates from the Mars Rover and the Saturn orbiter. Look—the captions help explain what you're looking at."

"Wow, it really *is* incredible," Danny said, watching the screen. "It's so much better than just seeing pictures in a book."

"Spectacular," Dad agreed. "We've come such a long way with technology. When I was born, we hadn't even landed on the moon yet."

"When you were born, people still thought it was made of cheese," Anna Mei teased him.

Dad clasped his chest as though deeply wounded. "Another blow to my rapidly waning youth."

"Hey," Danny said, sounding as though he'd just remembered something really important. "Did you guys hear that NASA decided not to open a restaurant on the moon after all?"

Anna Mei looked over at her father, who was already grinning in anticipation of the punch line he knew was coming. "Really? And why is that?"

"They figured that even if the food was good, the place wouldn't have much atmosphere."

Anna Mei remembered that one from the *Out of This World Joke Book* she'd read in the second grade, but Dad thought it was funny.

"While we're on the subject of food," he said, "I'm getting kind of hungry. What do you say we go and explore the cafeteria for a while?"

"Great!" Danny agreed, as if there'd been any doubt.

"You know what time astronauts always eat, don't you?" Dad asked him.

"No, when?" Danny asked.

"Launch time!"

While Danny groaned, Dad put his hand on his shoulder and steered him toward the exit.

Anna Mei would have liked to stay for a while longer, watching those incredible images shift and glow on the screen. But Danny and her father had already gone. She took one last look, then headed out the door behind them.

Chapter Seven

"My Very Best Cousin"

Anna Mei had hoped the weather would have cleared up by now, so she and Emily could go outside. But it was still raining, which meant she was stuck in Aunt Karen's living room for a while longer, doing whatever her cousin wanted. So far that included playing three different board games, doing four puzzles, and building a castle out of hundreds of little blocks.

Now they were reading Emily's favorite book, all about the adventures of red fish and blue fish. At age six she could read some of the words on her own. The rest she'd probably just memorized after hearing them so many times. Either way, after she insisted on reading it approximately thirty-seven times, Anna Mei couldn't take it anymore.

"Let's do something else for a while," she suggested. "How about picking out a movie for us watch?" A movie wouldn't require much effort, and would kill another hour, besides.

"I know!" Emily said. "Let's play dress up!"

She went down the hall and disappeared into her room. A minute later she was back, lugging a pile of clothes and some stuffed animals.

"Here," she said, handing Anna Mei a floppy green hat, red sparkly shoes, and a bright yellow feather boa. "You can wear these," she said.

Anna Mei pulled them on over her own clothes, trying not to think about how ridiculous she must look. Thank goodness Aunt Karen didn't have a mirror in the living room, so at least she didn't have to see herself like this.

"This is Charlotte and Bun Bun," Emily said, giving her an orange striped cat and a soft brown bunny. "They can be the children you bring to the party."

"Children?" Anna Mei asked. "Why aren't they my pets?"

"Because we're mommies in this game, and mommies have to have children."

Well, that point was hard to argue with, even if most mommies Anna Mei knew didn't walk around town wearing sequined tutus and fairy wings, like Emily.

But her cousin did seem a little mom-like when

she put her hand on her hip and said with a big sigh, "You have to *pretend*."

Pretend? That was something Anna Mei had some experience with, anyway. In fact, she'd gotten a little too good at it when she first moved here, and had tried so desperately to fit in. She even remembered being jealous of Emily and her brother Benjamin, who both had blond hair, blue eyes, and round rosy cheeks. In other words, *they* obviously belonged in this family. It had taken her a little time to figure out that what you looked like had practically nothing to do with who your family was.

"Okay, I can handle that," she told Emily. She cuddled the cat and bunny in her arms. "Oh, what cute children I have! And so soft, too!"

"And mine are Stripes and Jo Jo," Emily said, showing Anna Mei her tiger and teddy bear. "Stripes is the big sister, and Jo Jo is the little brother. And today is Jo Jo's birthday."

"Well, happy birthday, Jo Jo," Anna Mei said to the bear Emily was dressing in a cardboard party hat. "And how old are you today?"

Emily sighed again. "Of course he can't *talk*," she said, sounding tired of explaining things to her fancily-dressed yet obviously slow-witted visitor. "He's only one year old, just like Benjy. Only Jo Jo isn't sick with a tummy ache."

That tummy ache is what had landed Anna Mei here in the first place. Danny was coming over later for a movie night, so she had planned to spend the whole rainy day snuggling with Cleo in her comfy, striped chair, reading the next book on her list.

Then Mom had shown up with a favor to ask. She'd been talking with Aunt Karen, who had apparently been up all night with Benjamin. Now Aunt Karen was facing a long day with a sick toddler and a bored six-year-old.

"I told her I have to work today," Mom said. "But I thought it would be great if you could go over there and help out for a few hours. You know how much Emily loves playing with you, and maybe Aunt Karen could take a nap. It would really help them out."

Anna Mei felt her cozy afternoon slipping away. But how could she say no? Aunt Karen was always so nice to her. Besides, having the two families together had been the whole point of moving here in the first place.

"Okay," she agreed, "as long I'm back before Danny comes over."

"Thanks, honey," Mom said, reaching out to push Anna Mei's hair from her face, then bending down to kiss the top of her head. "I'll drop you off on my way to the hospital, and have your dad come and get you after work. If it's still raining, you guys could stop and pick up Danny, too."

It occurred to Anna Mei that they'd all gotten used to the fact that Danny would either ride his bike over or get a ride from the Andersons. No one ever talked about Anna Mei visiting Danny's, or even Danny getting dropped off by his parents or his brother. She wondered if anyone else noticed that.

"Now what do we do?" she asked Emily, who was busy pulling a bib over her bear's head.

"Now it's time for Jo Jo's birthday party," Emily announced.

"Okay, but make sure you don't feed him too much cake. We don't want *two* little brothers throwing up around here."

"We sure don't." Aunt Karen was coming down the hallway toward them. Only two years younger than Anna Mei's mother, she was a few inches shorter and wore her blond hair longer. Otherwise, the two women looked enough alike to be twins. "One sick little brother is plenty."

"Hi, Mommy!" Emily called out happily. At her mother's quick *shhhh*, she dropped her voice to a less dangerous decibel. "We're playing party, and it's Jo Jo's birthday."

"Sounds like you two are having a good time."

Emily nodded as she set her stuffed bear on the couch, propping him up with a pillow. "Anna Mei is my very best cousin," she declared.

Aunt Karen caught Anna Mei's eye and they both grinned. They had explained more than once that Anna Mei was Emily's *only* cousin, but that never seemed to affect Emily's rating system.

"I just can't tell you how much I appreciate your

coming over today," Aunt Karen said. "I feel so much better now that I've had some rest. And this is the longest Benjamin has slept in two days."

"That's okay," Anna Mei told her. "I didn't have any plans until later tonight."

"Oh right, your mom mentioned your plans with Danny. I'm looking forward to seeing him next week."

Anna Mei looked at her, puzzled. Had Danny somehow made plans with Aunt Karen and Uncle Jeff? Without telling her?

"When are you seeing Danny next week?" she asked.

"Well, I just assumed he'd be joining us for the picnic," Aunt Karen said. Anna Mei must have still looked blank, because she added, "The picnic we're all having on the Fourth of July, at the lake."

"Tell Danny to bring his squirt gun!" Emily said. She'd been at the Andersons' house once when Danny showed up, armed for another water fight. The two girls had ganged up against him and they all ended up soaking wet. Emily had gone home wrapped in one of Anna Mei's old sweatshirts and grinning from ear to ear.

Now her whole family had apparently started thinking of Danny as an honorary Anderson.

"Actually, I don't know if he's coming," she told them. "He might already have plans with his own family."

"Awww," Emily said, frowning.

"That's okay," Aunt Karen told her. "I'm sure we'll see him sometime soon. Listen, since Benjy is still sleeping, why don't we make some cupcakes for Jo Jo's birthday? Then Anna Mei can take some home for Aunt Margaret and Uncle Greg."

"And Danny, too?" Emily wanted to know.

"Of course Danny, too," her mother assured her.

"Yay! Can they be chocolate? With frosting?"

Emily followed her mother into the kitchen, taking her furry children with her.

Charlotte and Bun Bun were not so lucky. "Sorry, kids," Anna Mei said, "but this mommy is taking the rest of the day off." She left them sitting on the couch, right next to the floppy green hat, red sparkly shoes, and yellow feather boa.

Fireworks

As it turned out, Danny didn't already have plans for the Fourth. He showed up at their house in the morning, hauling a backpack filled with packages of hot dogs and buns, plus a tin of brownies.

"My mom sent them," he said, parking his bike in the garage where the Andersons were loading up their car. "She thinks you must be getting tired of feeding me all the time."

"Tired of it? Never," Anna Mei's father had assured him. He shoved a cooler over to make room for his fishing gear. "Going bankrupt from it? Well, that's another kettle of fish."

He chuckled at his own joke. "Kettle of fish—get it?"

Of course Danny had smiled, but just for a

second, Anna Mei thought she saw an expression of uncertainty flicker across his face.

Mom came out of the house carrying a beach bag full of towels and sunscreen lotion. "Are you sure we can't stop and pick up your parents on the way to the lake?" she asked Danny. "There's plenty of food, and we'd love to have them join us."

Say yes, Anna Mei thought. She wanted that weird feeling to go away—the one that kept telling her that Danny didn't want her anywhere near his parents.

"Thanks, but my dad has to work today, and my mom said she has stuff to catch up on at home."

"But it's a holiday," Anna Mei pointed out, then realized how dopey it sounded. "I mean, the university is closed today, right Dad?"

"I guess not for everyone," Dad said, packing the beach bag next to the picnic basket.

"Yeah, someone from maintenance has to be there all the time," Danny explained. "And they pay overtime on holidays, so my dad volunteered."

Anna Mei had to hand it to him—he was always ready with an explanation for why his parents were never available.

"Well, we're glad you're here, anyway," Mom said, smiling at him. "Greg, did you ever find your sunglasses?"

Finally ready, they piled in and drove over to Aunt Karen's house, where Uncle Jeff was buckling Emily and Benjamin into the backseat. Both kids were wearing red, white, and blue shirts and shorts. Benjamin, recovered now and back to his usual cheerful self, was smiling and waving an American flag out the window. Emily was doing the same with her star-spangled pinwheel, watching it spin in the breeze.

With Uncle Jeff's car in the lead, they headed out of town and along miles of bumpy country roads. Just when Anna Mei was sure they might end up in the official Middle of Nowhere, U.S.A., they pulled into a parking lot with a sign that said *Hillard's Lake*. It led to a grassy picnic area with plenty of tables, plus a dock and a nearby marina.

After helping push two tables together and unloading the car, Anna Mei walked through the picnic area so she could get a better view of the lake. The sandy beach was dotted with people in bright swimsuits and towels. The sunlight glinted and sparkled on the water, where waves from a passing motorboat lapped at the dock pilings.

"Not too shabby, huh?" Danny said, coming up behind her. "In fact, I'd say it's the perfect place to picnic," he said, deliberately exaggerating the *p*'s.

"You think so?" she asked, without turning to look at him.

"Sure—what more could you ask for?"

"Nothing, I guess," she said. But in her head, she had a different answer.

It was one of those summer days that seemed to last forever, as if even the sun wanted to stay out and play for as long as possible.

They went swimming first, wading in from the beach and then jumping off the dock. In a contest to see who could do the biggest cannonball, Uncle Jeff won hands down, splashing every swimmer within miles. He claimed he'd been practicing for the honor since he was Emily's age.

Anna Mei liked floating on her back, her face to the warm sun. Of course, as soon as her dad discovered that, he spent a lot of time disappearing underwater and sneaking up on her from below.

Danny, having grown up in the "Great Lakes State," swam like a fish. "I learned when I was a little kid," he told them, slicing through the water with more grace and skill than she ever suspected he had.

Mom and Aunt Karen stayed in the shallow water with Benjamin, but Emily had taken swimming lessons and was allowed to go out deeper with her father. Her favorite thing was jumping off the dock into his arms. She squealed just as loudly on the tenth jump as on the first.

When everyone got hungry, Dad started the charcoal grill while Danny and Anna Mei unpacked the food. After gathering at the table to say grace, they all started loading up their plates with grilled chicken, hot dogs, corn on the cob, and fruit salad. They finished it off with Mrs. Gallagher's brownies and Aunt Karen's flag cake. She had spread white frosting on the top, then arranged blueberries and strawberries into stars and stripes. It even had candles that sputtered like little firecrackers.

After lunch they went to the marina and rented a pontoon. It was slow moving but big enough for all of them to fit on together. They cruised the lake for a little while, then Dad dropped the anchor and got out the fishing poles.

Danny said he'd never fished much, but with Uncle Jeff's help he was soon baiting his own hook and casting his line. Anna Mei didn't mind handling the worms, but Emily wouldn't go near them, so Danny cheerfully took over bait duty for her, too. They caught a lot of little fish and only a few keepers, so in the end they just let them all go.

As soon as the sun started to go down, the fireflies came out. Some of the people around them had sparklers, which Emily said looked like magic wands waving in the air. Finally the sky grew dark enough for the official fireworks show to begin over the lake.

Benjamin lay in his mother's lap, worn out and sound asleep, but Emily sat with Anna Mei and Danny on a blanket, her wide blue eyes bright with excitement. At the first explosion she clapped and cheered.

"See, Mommy? I'm not afraid like when I was little!"

Anna Mei felt like cheering, too, watching the bursts of light shoot up through the night sky, all their bright color and dazzling sparkle reflected in the lake right at her feet. It was funny to think that the fireworks had probably come from China, just like she did.

She felt a surge of pride in the United States, the country she now called home. After all, it had welcomed not only her but her family's Danish and Swedish ancestors before her, and Danny's Irish ones, too.

She glanced over at Danny. His face, tipped up to the sky, was definitely sunburned, despite the layers of sunscreen he'd lathered on. Even more freckles seemed to have appeared on his nose, and he was absently munching on popcorn as he watched.

The day had been so much fun, partly because Danny had been there to share it. But she just couldn't shake the feeling that something was wrong. Here he was spending all this time with her family—even celebrating holidays with them—and yet, he'd never once invited her over to his house. It seemed like he was deliberately keeping her away. But why?

"Ow, that one's too loud!" Emily said, as one of the rockets cracked the sky with a roaring boom. "It hurts my ears."

Anna Mei was about to explain that a noise couldn't hurt her when Danny reached over and put his arm around Emily's shoulder.

"Don't worry," he said to her. "I can tell when that kind is coming. We'll cover our ears together, okay?"

Emily nodded and scooted closer to him, where she stayed until the show was over and it was time to pack up and leave for home.

"Thanks for inviting me," Danny said, when they dropped him off at his house. "I had a—"

"Don't tell me," Dad interrupted. "A blast?"

Danny grinned. "Yeah, a blast."

Climbing out of the car, he assured the Andersons that his parents would already have gone to bed, so there was no point inviting them to come inside.

Chapter Nine

Not So Easy to Fix

Danny's sunburn had faded to a light pink by the time Anna Mei saw him a few days later. They met at the nature center, about halfway between their houses, and now were sitting on their favorite bench near the pond. Their bikes and helmets lay on the grass nearby.

Anna Mei had her notebook open to the page of observations she'd jotted down during their last visit.

Lots of red birds today. Are all red birds cardinals?

2 different kinds of turtles in pond. Smaller one has red trim along edge of shell. Bigger one has yellow stripes on neck & legs, speckles on shell. Try to identify.

3 sandhill cranes swooped down & grabbed bugs from pond. One crane much smaller than the others—could this be a family?

Danny had already sketched some of the wildlife they'd seen. Anna Mei planned to scan his drawings into her computer, add some of her research, and then print out a kind of guide to animal life at the center.

"Is it for extra credit?" Danny asked, the first day she'd described her idea. "We don't even know who our seventh grade science teacher is yet."

"I'm just interested," she'd told him. "I like seeing what animals do when you just sit quietly and leave them alone."

"You mean besides eat and sleep?"

She laughed. He really had a way of boiling everything down to the basics. "Yeah, besides that. Observation is a very important part of science, you know. I need to get really good at it. I also think it would be fun to get a job here someday. Did you notice that the counselors running the kids' camps are high school students?"

He hadn't noticed, but he did agree that it would be cool for them to have jobs here when they were old enough. He also agreed to sketch the wildlife for her project, even though it wasn't exactly the kind of artwork he was interested in.

But today she was the one who just wasn't interested in the project. She had a headache, for one thing, and her eyes felt itchy. Maybe she was allergic to the pollen or something in the air.

Or maybe her mood had something to do with the argument she'd had with her mother this morning. Anna Mei had been in the kitchen, minding her own business and packing lunches for herself and Danny, when Mom came up from the basement with a basket of laundry.

"Good morning," she had said, setting the basket down on a chair. "I was just about to—"

Then she noticed the food. "Why are you making lunch?" she asked. "I thought we'd go out to eat, maybe try that new deli that just opened downtown."

Anna Mei was confused. Her plans for the day involved biking to the nature center and eating lunch there with Danny, then coming home to watch a DVD he'd checked out at the library. It was a movie that had just come out and he was pretty excited about it.

But when she explained that, Mom had not been happy.

"It's my day off, Anna Mei," she said. "We were going to do something together, remember?"

She remembered *now*, but Danny was probably already on his way over. It was too late to call him and cancel.

"Sorry, Mom," she said. "We'll have to go out for lunch on your next day off."

She figured her mother would sigh, maybe say something about Anna Mei forgetting her own head if it wasn't attached. Then she'd get out her calendar so they could pick another day.

Instead, Mom had just looked at her for a minute, saying nothing. Then she'd picked up the basket and carried it upstairs. A few minutes later, Anna Mei heard her calling a friend and making plans with *her* for lunch and a movie.

So really, it had all worked out. They could both hang out with a friend today, and then do something together another time. No big deal.

Anna Mei closed her eyes and rubbed her temples. That stupid headache just wouldn't go away.

"What's wrong?" Danny asked. He had his sketchbook out but had stopped drawing.

"Nothing really," she said. "My mom got ticked off at me this morning, and it's still bugging me for some reason."

"Well, your mom's pretty cool. I'm sure she won't stay mad for long."

"Really?" Anna Mei said, suddenly feeling upset with him, too. Who did he think he was, explaining her own mother to her? The words flew out of her mouth before she could stop them. "So now you know more about my mom than I do?"

"What?" he asked, sounding bewildered. "I was just trying to help. But it's fine if you'd rather not talk about it."

"Actually, I think we *should* talk about it," she said. She set her notebook down on the bench and turned to face him. "Let's talk about mothers. In fact, let's talk about *your* mother."

"Mine?" he asked. "Why? What's she got to do with this?"

"Well, I wouldn't know, would I? I don't know a single thing about her, after all. Except that she likes to make brownies, I guess."

Danny stared at her without answering. Why did everyone keep doing that today? "And I'll bet she doesn't know much about me, either, right?" Anna Mei said, more as a statement than a question. Her head was really throbbing now. She put her hands up to her temples again.

Danny unzipped his backpack, then stuffed his sketchbook inside.

"We should try this again when you're feeling better," he said.

Anna Mei let out a breath that seemed to take all her anger with it. She suddenly just felt tired.

"But what about the movie?" she asked, watching him pick up his bike and climb on. Now that he was going, she wished she could go back and start over.

"Next time," he said.

"Danny, I—just forget what I said, okay? This headache is really bugging me."

"Don't worry about it," he said, but his voice

sounded strange, like it was coming from farther away than he actually was. "I hope you feel better soon."

"Really, Danny, I—"

"It's okay, I should go now anyway. See you later."

Watching him go, she hoped it *would* be okay. She really did. But as she rode her bike home by herself, she couldn't help wondering if she'd accidentally broken something today—something that might not be so easy to fix.

Chapter Ten

A Perfect Plan

On Saturday, Anna Mei's father asked if Danny was sick or away on vacation—he hadn't been around since the Fourth of July, over a week ago. Her mother wondered if Danny might like to join them for dinner tomorrow. She was planning to make mushroom-stuffed meatloaf, one of his favorites.

But when Anna Mei called to invite him, Danny said that he'd be busy helping his dad and Connor get the outside of their house ready for painting. He didn't sound mad at her exactly, but the conversation did seem a little flat and off-balance. She tried to liven things up by mentioning his birthday, which was coming up next week.

"We'll have to think of something really special to do," she said. "Go on a hot air balloon ride or something."

He didn't laugh or make a joke about knocking her out of the basket, or accidentally sailing off to Oz. He just said he'd be spending his birthday at his grandparents' house down in Indiana. He had aunts and uncles and cousins there, too, so it would probably be a pretty big group.

Finally they hung up without making any plans at all.

On Sunday, after an early breakfast of Dad's blueberry pancakes, the Andersons made the short drive to St. Joseph's for ten o'clock Mass. This church was much newer—and much smaller—than St. Cecelia's back in Boston. But it was closer to their house than St. Brigid's, the historic stone church downtown where the Gallaghers went. Luis's family belonged to St. Joseph's, too, and Anna Mei often saw him and his sister altar serving together.

Today she sat in a pew between her parents, just as she'd done ever since she was a baby. Her mother turned her hymnal toward Anna Mei so they could share, and hugged her during the Sign of Peace, just like always. Obviously Mom wasn't carrying a grudge about what had happened between them.

If she can get over it, why can't Danny? Anna Mei wondered. *Besides, what did I do to deserve the silent treatment, anyway? Was it a crime to ask a simple question about his mother? Really, he was the one acting all weird about the whole thing. If I can just get him to lighten up a little, maybe I could make him see that. And then maybe he would—*

She was startled when her father nudged her to stand and join the line for Communion. The Mass was nearly over and all she'd done was worry about Danny. She obviously could use a little help here.

Back in the pew again, she rested her head in her hands and closed her eyes.

You've given me so much already, she prayed, *and I'm truly grateful. But now I need help figuring out what to do about Danny—how can I get things to be normal again between us?*

Although praying always made Anna Mei feel better, she had learned not to expect easy or instant answers. But later in the day, during a phone conversation with Zandra, she had an inspiration. They'd started out talking about volleyball camp, and then Zandra had said that even though she was having a good summer, she missed seeing everyone. She thought they should all try to get together sometime.

Just like in the cartoons, a light bulb seemed to go off over Anna Mei's head. "Danny's birthday!" she said. "Let's do something for that."

"When is it?" Zandra asked.

"Next Sunday, but he'll be out of town that day. We could have a party on Saturday instead, and surprise him."

Zandra, who loved a party for any reason, jumped right on it. "Just tell me how I can help," she said.

That night, Anna Mei grabbed her notebook and pencil before pulling back the covers on her bed. Cleo, who Anna Mei suspected could hear the sound of a pillow being fluffed up from three miles away, appeared at the door, ready for bedtime.

"Not quite yet," Anna Mei told her. "I have to plan Danny's party first."

Her own twelfth birthday was last January, when she was still pretty new here. Some of the kids at school sang "Happy Birthday" to her at lunch, and she'd gotten a few e-mails from her old friends in Boston. She'd figured that this, along with some gifts from her parents, would be the extent of the celebration.

But her mother had thought otherwise. Later she told Anna Mei that a girl only turns twelve once, and that she deserves to have more fun than two creaky old parents could provide, or something like that. It had been her idea to call Zandra and ask her to invite all the girls on the volleyball team to the Andersons' for a sleepover on Friday night. So when Anna Mei and her father had come home from running an errand, the girls were already there, ready to surprise her.

Now Anna Mei sat back against her pillow, her bent knees making a little table for her notebook. "It's a perfect plan," she said to Cleo, who had jumped up beside her and was poking her nose into the covers, looking for a place to burrow.

She turned to a new page and wrote at the top.

Danny's Surprise Party

This would work, she was sure of it. Once they were all together—Zandra, Luis, Danny and her—Danny would act like himself again, and everything would be back to normal.

Chapter Eleven

The Birthday Rule

"You've got to be kidding!" Anna Mei said, watching in disbelief as Zandra bowled her third spare in a row. "You could have told me you were a pro when we decided to have Danny's party here."

Zandra smiled and shrugged. "You didn't ask me if I was any good at it," she said. "You just asked if I thought it would be fun."

Danny got up to take his turn next. "If only you could spare *me* from having to go after you and make a fool of myself," he told her. "Unless watching me do that is where the fun part comes in."

Anna Mei laughed, not really at his joke, but because she was relieved that he sounded like the old Danny again—even if the old Danny was turning out to be a pretty terrible bowler.

She had thought of coming here because she missed bowling with her friends. Back in Boston, they'd played "candlepin." The pins were tall and skinny instead of bottle-shaped like the ones they had here, where the game was ten-pin. And the balls she had used were much smaller and lighter than these were. She had to try out a couple of different ones before she got the hang of it.

Still, it was basically the same game—all you had to do was aim the ball at the pins. After that it was a simple matter of physics and mechanics.

But poor Danny had never bowled much before. When they first started, he joked with the attendant that he would need a bumper lane, the kind little kids used to keep their balls out of the gutter. Quite a few gutter balls later, he had the lowest score by far.

"Actually Danny, the fun part is being together on your birthday," Zandra told him. "Well, not technically *on* your birthday, since it's not until tomorrow. But you know what I mean."

"And besides," Luis said, "there's that special rule."

"What rule?" Anna Mei asked, suspiciously. Although Luis's face had a serious expression, she'd caught the hint of a sparkle in his dark eyes.

"You know—the birthday rule," he said. "Whenever you're bowling to celebrate a birthday, the person with the *lowest* score always wins. I thought everyone knew that."

"Oh, sure," Danny said, reaching for the neon green bowling ball he'd chosen from the rack earlier. "That doesn't sound suspicious at all."

"Hey, it's in the rule book—look it up," Luis insisted.

Always a team player, Zandra happily jumped aboard the "Special Birthday Rule" Express. "Well, *I* certainly knew about it. That's why I'm trying so hard to let Danny win."

Danny set the ball back down, then posed with his hand placed reverently over his heart. "And I want you all to know that I'm deeply, deeply touched by your thoughtfulness."

"No problem," Luis assured him. "We figure it's cheaper than a present."

Anna Mei shared in their laughter as Danny finally stepped forward to take his turn.

She was so relieved that everything was going exactly as she had planned. She'd been worried that Danny would make an excuse not to come over today, even though she told him her parents wanted to give him a gift. So she'd put her mother on the phone to invite him herself.

Then when Danny showed up, Dad came out to the driveway, saying he needed something from the grocery store for the dinner he was making. Anna Mei had practically jumped into the car, dragging Danny with her.

But instead of the grocery store, they drove to the bowling alley where Anna Mei's mother had reserved the special events room. Zandra and Luis were already there—they'd come early to decorate the room with balloons, crepe paper, and a banner that said "Danny's Turning 12 . . . and That's No Blarney." They'd even put little shamrock stickers all over it.

"Wow," Danny had said, looking wide-eyed at the decorations, the stack of presents, and the chocolate frosted cake arranged on a table. "This is so nice of you guys."

"It was Anna Mei's idea," Zandra told him. "Luis and I are just the little worker bees."

Danny had turned to Anna Mei and smiled. "I really didn't expect anything like this. Thanks."

She knew him well enough to know that this was for real.

"You're welcome," she said, her smile as wide as his. "Happy birthday."

They bowled for over an hour, with Danny "winning" the whole time. He was a good sport about it, though, cheering the others on and mocking his own lack of skills.

Then they headed back to the events room to eat. The rental deal included pizza for six, but Anna Mei had figured that four twelve-year-olds could eat as much as six, especially if one of them was Danny Gallagher. And if anything was left over, Dad could have it when he came to pick them up.

While they waited for the pizza, Danny got busy opening his gifts. Zandra's was a new sketchpad and some charcoal pencils. Luis gave him a Detroit Redwings hockey jersey—he and Danny were both lifelong fans.

Anna Mei couldn't wait for him to see her gift. She had found it online a few weeks ago and her mother had helped with the ordering. Now she watched Danny tear the bright wrapping paper off the box and unfold the black T-shirt.

"Those symbols on the front are Japanese. They mean *peace* and *courage*," she explained. "But the best part is the back."

He flipped the shirt over where the phrase *Anime Rules* was written in big white letters.

"It's to remind you that no matter how you spell it," she said, "*Anna Mei* rules."

"As if you'd ever let me forget it," he answered, rolling his eyes at her. But he was smiling as he folded the shirt and put it back in the box.

In the end they managed to eat most of the pizza and half of the cake. Even Danny said he couldn't handle another bite. They talked about getting together again and started comparing schedules. Zandra and Anna Mei would both be away at camp soon. Luis said his family had plans to go to an amusement park in Sandusky, Ohio—they were all big roller coaster fans. And Anna Mei's trip to Boston was still scheduled for sometime in August.

"What about you, Danny?" Zandra asked. "Is your family going on vacation, too?"

Danny hesitated a moment, then just shrugged. "Who knows?" he said casually. "They never tell me anything until the last minute. I'll be lucky if I have time to pack a suitcase before the car pulls out of the driveway."

It was no answer at all—Anna Mei wondered if anyone else noticed that.

Zandra had started taking down the banner and crepe paper. "You must have special plans for tomorrow, though," she said.

"Just dinner at home," he told her. "My mom is making all my favorite foods."

"Your poor mom—that means she's going to be in the kitchen all day," Luis said.

Danny laughed but Anna Mei frowned. "But you said—I mean, what happened to Indiana? The grandparents and the cousins?"

He answered without looking at her. In fact, he appeared to be suddenly fascinated by watching Zandra and Luis peel tape off the wall. "That didn't work out after all. But it's okay—I don't mind it being just my family. We'll have a good time."

And there it was again—that big, heavy door slamming shut against the possibility of her getting anywhere near the Gallaghers. She hadn't been imagining it. She really wasn't welcome at his house, not even on his birthday.

She felt her cheeks growing hot with anger. But she didn't want to confront him now, not with Zandra and Luis here. Without answering, she got up and started throwing cups and napkins into the trash.

"What should we do with these?" Luis asked. He pointed to the twelve blue and red helium balloons floating overhead, their long ribbons anchored to the tablecloth with tape.

"I could take some home for my brothers and sister," Zandra said.

"And I'll take three for my sisters," Luis said. "Do you want the rest, Danny?"

He didn't, so Luis and Zandra ended up popping them and throwing them away.

It doesn't matter, Anna Mei told herself. *This party's over anyway.*

But it still bothered her somehow. Just a few minutes ago, the balloons had been all bright and bouncy, dancing around on their colorful strings. Now they were just tattered pieces of junk, lying on top of some crumpled up napkins in the trash.

Chapter Twelve

What About Me?

A few days later, Anna Mei sat at the table, pushing food around her plate but not really eating it.

Mom and Dad were both home for dinner, which didn't happen every day. When they lived in Boston, her mother had worked at a doctor's office with daytime hours. Now that she worked at a hospital, her shifts were noon to midnight three times a week. So sometimes it was just Anna Mei and her father sitting at the table, or Anna Mei, her father, and Danny—although that hadn't happened for a few weeks now.

Tonight she couldn't stop thinking about the bowling party, and how happy she'd been when everything had seemed okay. Now she almost felt worse than before. Did Danny think she wouldn't notice how secretive he was being about his family? Did he think she wouldn't care?

"Are you all right, Anna Mei?" Mom asked, looking at the uneaten spaghetti piled on Anna Mei's plate.

"I'm fine," she said. "Still full from lunch, I guess."

"Well, at least eat your salad," Mom said, passing her a bottle of ranch dressing. "Dad and I have something we want to talk to you about."

Great. Now they were going to ask her why Danny hadn't been around lately, and she was going to have to figure out what to say.

"It's about my trip to Seattle," Dad said, helping himself to a piece of garlic bread.

Seattle? Anna Mei relaxed. She already knew that Dad would be attending a conference at the University of Washington this summer. Actually, he would be presenting some of his research there, which she thought was pretty cool.

"When is it?" she asked. Maybe he was going to invite her to come along—that would be even cooler.

"That's what we want to talk to you about," he said. "It turns out that the conference dates overlap with your week at volleyball camp."

"Oh." *So much for a trip to Seattle*. "Then I guess you'll be here by yourself that week, Mom."

"Actually," her mother said, "I've decided to take a few days off and go with your dad. We thought it would be a good chance for him to show me the great Northwest."

Dad had some cousins on the west coast and had been to Seattle a couple of times before. "I'm going to do my best tour guide impersonation," he said. "For example, that tall, skinny tower is the Space Needle, and the big wet thing where the road ends? That's the Pacific Ocean."

Anna Mei had to smile. "It sounds like fun," she said. "But if we're all gone at the same time, who's going to be here with Cleo?"

Mom got up to bring the coffee pot over to the table. "Actually, we have a bigger problem," she said, filling her cup and then pouring some for Dad.

"We do?" Anna Mei asked.

"The conference starts on Monday the twenty-eighth," Dad said, "the same day as camp. But your mom and I want to leave on the Friday before, so we can spend the weekend sightseeing."

"Then . . . what would I do between Friday and Monday?"

"I've asked Aunt Karen and Uncle Jeff if you can stay with them," Mom said. "I'm sure Emily and Benjamin will love it."

Well, moving in with two energetic little kids wouldn't be Anna Mei's first choice, but it was pretty clear that her parents weren't asking her opinion. She would have to stay *somewhere* over the weekend. She supposed she could handle it for a few days.

"Okay," she said. "I just have to be at the bus station early Monday morning."

"That's the part we still have to figure out," Mom said. "Uncle Jeff might have to work an early shift that day, so Aunt Karen wouldn't have a car to use. I was thinking I could loan them my car while we're gone."

"Or I could ask Zandra for a ride—she'll be going to the bus station anyway," Anna Mei suggested.

"That's a good idea," Dad said. "If Zandra's parents could help us out, we'd be all set."

Cleo, lurking under the table as she always did during a meal, meowed at just that moment. To Anna Mei it sounded exactly like, *Hey, what about me?*

"Wait a minute," she said, "that doesn't solve the problem about Cleo. Emily told me that Uncle Jeff is allergic to cats, so I can't take her with me."

"I forgot about that," Mom said. She sipped her coffee while Dad finished his second helping of spaghetti. "I suppose Cleo will have to stay here. Aunt Karen can come over once a day to feed her. The kids will like that."

"But Cleo will *hate* it." Anna Mei pushed her plate of uneaten spaghetti away. "She'll be so lonely here all by herself. She won't know what's happened to us."

"Well, we obviously still have some details to work out," Dad said. He got up and started stacking the dishes. "Let's talk about it again later, when we've all had time to put our minds to it."

While Dad carried the dishes to the sink and Mom started putting leftovers away, Anna Mei ducked under the table to scoop Cleo into her arms. "Don't worry," she said softly, rubbing her cheek against the soft, gray fur. "I'll think of some way to take care of you, I promise."

In the end it was actually Zandra who came up with a solution. When Anna Mei called to ask her about a ride to the bus, Zandra insisted that Anna Mei and Cleo both come and stay at her house for the weekend. Her family would take care of Cleo until Thursday, when Anna Mei's parents returned from Seattle and came to pick the cat up.

"That's really nice of you, Zandra, but . . . are you sure?" Anna Mei asked, hesitantly.

The truth was—*she* wasn't sure. She liked Zandra, of course, and Zandra's parents seemed nice enough. But staying with a family she barely knew for three days? Maybe she'd be better off at Aunt Karen's after all.

"Oh my gosh, we'll have so much fun!" Zandra said, sounding excited enough for both of them. "Aleesha can sleep on the pull-out couch in the living room, so we'll have my room all to ourselves. Just think—the whole weekend together and then we get to go to camp, too. I'll talk to my mom right now and call you back, okay?"

Anna Mei barely had time to run the idea past her own parents before the phone rang again. The next thing she knew, Mom had talked with Mrs. Caine and the whole thing was a done deal.

"They seem very sincere about it," Mom said, after hanging up the phone. "I'm sure this will be more fun for you than staying at Aunt Karen's. And it will be better for Cleo, too. We'll just drop you both off on our way to the airport."

"Great," Anna Mei said, hoping she sounded enthusiastic enough.

On the bright side, even if it wasn't exactly *great*, at least it would give her something to think about besides Danny for a change.

Chapter Thirteen

The Caine Family Circus

"Really, Zandra," Anna Mei asked, "don't you ever feel like you're living in the middle of a sitcom?"

Zandra laughed as she closed her bedroom door for about the twentieth time, trying to keep her brothers and sister on the other side of it. Her success rate so far was zero, as one after the other had trooped in asking for help with something, or wanting her to play with them, or just demanding to know what she and Anna Mei were doing in there.

"I guess I'm just used to it," Zandra said. "I was only two years old when Aleesha was born, so I don't even remember a time when I wasn't a big sister."

Cleo had taken refuge under Aleesha's bed, as skittish about all the noise and commotion as her owner. Anna Mei had given up trying to coax her out for now. The peace and quiet probably wouldn't last long anyway—Cleo might as well enjoy it.

The two girls were sprawled across Zandra's bed, looking through a pile of sports magazines Zandra had pulled out of her closet. One of them featured members of the U.S. Women's Indoor Volleyball Team, who had taken the silver medal in the Beijing Olympics.

"For inspiration," Zandra had said, handing that one to Anna Mei.

"They are pretty amazing," Anna Mei agreed, as she flipped through page after page of player photos and statistics. "But did you happen to notice the tiny little detail that they're all about six feet tall? Maybe I should be going to gymnastics camp instead."

"Oh, come on," Zandra said. "You may not be tall but you're really quick. And look—" she pointed at the stats for a player from California, "this one's only five foot four. If she can do it, so can you."

"Easy for you to say—you're already almost that tall. Not to mention better at sports than anyone I know."

It was true—Zandra not only had the muscular build of a natural athlete, she always moved with energy and purpose, even if she was just walking across the room. And her attitude was so positive, as if she never had any doubts or hesitation. If something needed to be done, she just went ahead and did it.

You never had to worry about her backing you up, on the court or anywhere else. Anna Mei thought that was a pretty great quality to have in a friend.

She turned another page and found an article about the city of Beijing itself, filled with images of towering skyscrapers and majestic temples. But it was the sunny, green parks blooming with cherry and plum trees that made her breath catch in her throat. Her birth mother had named her Mei Li—"beautiful plum blossom." And although Beijing was a long way from the Hunan province where she'd been born, Anna Mei felt a sense of wonder that she had started out her life in a country so beautiful and mysterious.

"Do you think you'd ever want to go there?" Zandra asked, looking over Anna Mei's shoulder at the photo spread. "Just out of curiosity?"

Anna Mei nodded. "Maybe someday," she said. "My parents would like to go back and visit, so they could show me the orphanage in Yiyang. My birth mother probably lived somewhere around there. I think it would—"

She was interrupted by the sound of someone knocking on the door.

"I told you guys—we're busy right now!" Zandra called out to whichever brother or sister wouldn't take no for an answer.

But when the door opened it was Zandra's mother, holding a carton of milk and two glasses. Eight-year-old R.J., the older of the two Caine boys, followed close behind with a plate of cookies.

"Sorry to interrupt," she told the girls, setting the glasses down on Zandra's dresser. "R.J. and I have been busy in the kitchen, and I thought I'd better bring you some cookies before they're all gone. You know that sweets don't last long around here."

"Thanks, Mom," Zandra said. She rolled off the bed and went to take the plate from her brother. "Did you help make these, R.J.?" she asked, bending down to hug him. "You did a great job!"

R.J.'s smile was like a miniature version of Zandra's. But when Anna Mei caught his eye, he quickly looked away.

Zandra had told her that R.J. was autistic, but Anna Mei didn't really know how that worked. He seemed fine to her, although he was certainly quieter than the rest of the Caine kids. And he didn't go to Elmwood Elementary—his school was in a different district, where he had a special tutor.

"I hope you're not allergic to peanuts, Anna Mei," Mrs. Caine said. "Peanut butter cookies are R.J.'s favorite."

Anna Mei shook her head. "I'm not," she said. "These look great. And thanks again for inviting me, Mrs. Caine. I know you have a lot going on already."

Mrs. Caine opened the milk and started pouring it into the glasses. "If that's a polite way of saying I have my hands full with this rowdy bunch, you're right," she said. "But I love having lots of kids around. I always said I would either have a big family someday, or run a day care center."

Zandra grinned. "Dad says you do both."

"I guess that's true," Mrs. Caine said with a chuckle. "But you're all good kids. I know I'm blessed to have this family, even if I do feel like the ring master at a circus sometimes. And as for you, Anna Mei, you are welcome at the Caine family circus any time. No charge, refreshments included."

When Mrs. Caine went back downstairs, R.J. stayed behind. He pulled Zandra toward him and whispered something in her ear.

"Okay," Zandra told him, "let's ask her together."

Holding hands, they came over to the bed where Anna Mei was sitting. "R.J. and I were wondering if it would be all right for him to pet Cleo," Zandra said. "He promises to be very gentle."

"Actually, I think Cleo would like that," Anna Mei said.

She went over to Aleesha's bed and peered underneath. "Here, kitty," she coaxed, holding out her hand. "Come on out, Cleo. There's someone who wants to meet you."

In a few minutes the cat was sitting in Anna Mei's lap while R.J. pet her. When she started purring, R.J.'s grin practically lit up the room.

"He's really sweet, isn't he?" Anna Mei said, looking up at Zandra.

Zandra nodded. "Most of the time," she said. "It's just that you never know when something's going to set him off. And when that happens—stand back."

Anna Mei couldn't imagine that, but before she could ask Zandra to explain, the sound of pounding feet came from the stairs again. Aleesha burst into the room, followed by five-year-old Marcus, the youngest brother. Cleo burrowed deeper into Anna Mei's arms, trying to hide.

"Come on, Zannie," Aleesha said. "We want to play with you guys, too!"

"Yeah, come on!" Marcus pleaded.

R.J. turned to face them, no longer smiling. "Stop it, you're scaring the kitty!"

Zandra sighed. "There's probably no escape this time," she said to Anna Mei. "Let's go play kickball or something for a while. We can come back up here later, when they're getting ready for bed."

"I don't mind," Anna Mei said, and realized she really didn't. It was kind of fun being around so much noise and activity for a change.

Zandra calmed R.J. by offering him a cookie and promising he could be on her team. He stroked Cleo one last time before Anna Mei set her down and she disappeared under the bed again. Unlike Anna Mei, the cat seemed to have no plans to join the Caine family circus any time soon.

Stepping Up

Just as Zandra had predicted, volleyball camp turned out to be a blast.

When they first got on the bus, they only knew a few other girls—those who had been on their team at Elmwood or had played for other area schools. But with Zandra around, meeting people was never a problem. By the time the bus arrived at camp four hours later, they knew practically everyone on it. And by dinnertime, they had met dozens more girls from all over the state.

The camp was being held at a college campus. Their coaches doubled as counselors, keeping an eye on things whether the girls were on the court or off. They were mostly college students who had played volleyball in high school; some were still on club teams or travel teams.

The days were filled with plenty of games and matches, of course, with the coaches mixing things up so that someone who was a teammate this time might be an opponent next time. But playing was only part of the program—the rest had to do with working on new skills and physical conditioning. The coaches said no one could play without stamina, and there was no other way to get it than by running miles of sprints and doing loads of calisthenics.

The other thing they kept drilling was the importance of teamwork, and being there for each other during a game. "Volleyball is like all team sports," one of the coaches explained on the very first day. "You have to be willing to step up and make the play, of course, but you also have to step up for your fellow players—really be there for them when they're struggling to reach the ball or move into a block. Stay alert so you're ready with support as soon as it's needed."

It was a lot of work, and at night in her dorm room, Anna Mei practically fell into bed. She was more tired than she'd ever been in her life. But it was the kind of tired that made you feel like you'd really done something, and that you wouldn't mind doing it again the next day.

Mealtimes were always fun, with all the girls chatting nonstop while they loaded up on fruit and carbs in the huge cafeteria. And in the evenings the counselors encouraged them to bond by watching movies and playing games together.

For Anna Mei, camp felt like being in a whole different world, far from her ordinary life. She talked with her parents on the phone a couple of times, but it seemed strange knowing they were two thousand miles away. They were really enjoying Seattle, but said they missed her and would be there to meet her bus on Saturday.

Zandra reported that Cleo was doing fine at the Caine house. Her mother said that although the cat still preferred to stay in Zandra and Aleesha's room, she didn't run and hide anymore if someone came near. She seemed to have formed a special attachment to R.J.

As for Danny . . . well, he seemed pretty far away, too. Sometimes Zandra would mention him, or something funny would happen and Anna Mei would think, *I can't wait to tell Danny about that!* But then she would think about that day at the nature center, or the way he had avoided meeting her eyes at the bowling alley. Those memories stabbed at her and she had to push them away.

She had come to camp to have fun and improve her game. The stuff with Danny would just have to wait until she had time to figure it all out. After all, he would still be there when she got back, right?

Chapter Fifteen

Going Nowhere

As promised, her parents were waiting at the bus station on Saturday to pick her up. Dad accused her of growing half a foot in the week they had been apart, then laughed and admitted it was probably more like half a centimeter. Mom hugged her for what seemed like a very long time before wanting to hear every single detail about camp.

Back at home they gave her a souvenir they'd picked out in the Chinatown-International District—a framed Chinese brush painting of plum blossoms.

"I love it," she told them, holding the painting up and admiring the way a dozen shades of pink all blended together to bring the delicate blossoms to life. "It's going to look great in my room."

Later they all gathered in the basement family room so they could watch a slideshow of their trip.

Dad hooked up his laptop to the TV and sat nearby so he could point out every detail. Mom sat next to Anna Mei on the couch, providing backup narration. And Cleo had claimed her usual spot in Anna Mei's lap. In fact, she'd been like Anna Mei's shadow all afternoon. Apparently the cat's joy at their reunion had overcome any abandonment issues she may have been harboring.

The slideshow was interesting at first, but after what seemed like a hundred pictures of Seattle, Anna Mei started to get bored.

"Wow, how many pictures did you guys take?" she asked.

"Possibly a few more than we needed," Dad admitted. "Apparently, the Space Needle looks pretty much the same, no matter what angle you take the picture from."

He clicked through even more of those until the image finally changed. "Oh, here's one we took at the pier," he said.

"I really liked it there," Mom said. "Watching all the boats going in and out reminded me of Boston."

"And here's one of the fishmongers at Pike Place Market," Dad said. "The picture doesn't do it justice—they actually pick up those slippery fish and throw them across the store to each other. They're pretty good at catching them, too. I guess the alternative would be getting whacked in the face with a ten pound salmon."

"Gee, I'm so sorry I missed that," Anna Mei said, in a voice that clearly meant otherwise.

"The thing is, you would have liked it, Anna Mei," Mom said. "I know it sounds kind of silly, but every time we saw something new, I wanted to show it to you. It felt so strange not to have you with us."

"I felt that way, too," Dad said, as yet another picture of fish piled on an icy countertop flashed on the screen. "We haven't been on a trip without you since . . . well, since we went to China to adopt you."

"But we're going to Boston soon," Anna Mei reminded them. "We'll all be together then."

Her parents exchanged one of those glances that meant *okay, who's going to tell her?* Dad must have been elected in some kind of secret vote because he said, "I'm afraid that trip might have to go on hold for a little while. Even though the conference was work-related, it put me behind at the lab. I'm not sure I can get away again so soon."

"What do you mean?" Anna Mei asked, frowning. "Why don't they just hire more people?"

"It's not that simple, Anna Mei. These are my projects—I can't just hand them off to someone else."

"Then they'll just have to wait until we get back. What's wrong with that?"

Mom tried to smooth things over. "We know you were looking forward to seeing your friends," she said, "but your dad's work is important, too. We'll go to Boston as soon as we can, I promise."

Anna Mei felt her good mood growing sour. Exactly how was it fair that Mom and Dad's trip to Seattle meant that she didn't get to go to Boston? She and Lauren had already started making plans. And now the whole thing was being postponed until who knows when. To parents, "as soon as we can" could mean anything.

At least Dad was finally clicking off the slideshow. But then he said, "Speaking of friends, I'm surprised Danny hasn't been over here yet. You've already been home for . . . what? Four hours now?"

Great—now she had this to deal with, too. Not that she was surprised. After all, her parents were used to having Danny around a lot, so they were bound to wonder what was going on. But until she had a good answer to that question, she would just have to stall.

"Yeah, I need to call him," she said, trying to make her voice sound casual. "He's been really busy helping his dad paint their house."

She kept her eyes down, as if scratching Cleo behind the ears suddenly required her complete attention. Maybe they would see how busy she was and decide to talk about something else.

"Well, when you talk to him," Mom said, "don't make any plans for tomorrow afternoon. We thought it would be fun to go to that new art gallery in Langston, and then have dinner at a restaurant along the river. The weather is supposed to be just beautiful."

Whew. It looked like she was off the hook on the subject of Danny, at least for now.

"But I already did make plans," she said, "with Zandra. Her whole family is going to the community pool tomorrow, and they asked me to come."

Once again Anna Mei had no trouble decoding the glance between her parents—they obviously weren't very happy with the idea. She hurried to add, "If that's okay."

After an uncomfortable pause Dad said, "First of all, we'd appreciate your talking with us *before* you make plans, instead of after."

"I know—I'm sorry," she agreed, anxious to get past the apology part so she could move on to the permission part. "But it sort of happened when I was at their house last weekend. They said they wanted to do something fun when Zandra and I came home. Then once we were at camp I just forgot to tell you about it."

When neither of them answered, Anna Mei added, "But you guys can still go. To the art gallery, I mean."

Another pause. Was there some big deal about her being with Zandra tomorrow? After all, they were the ones who'd sent her to the Caines' in the first place, when *they* had wanted to make plans.

Finally Mom said, "I guess we'll have to decide that. But either way, I want you to keep in touch, and let us know when you're coming home. You can take my cell phone for the day."

"Okay," Anna Mei said. "And I'll be home in time for dinner tomorrow, I promise."

Dad was unplugging the laptop cord and winding it up. "See if Danny can come then," he said. "I've missed having him around lately."

"Sure," she said, flashing a smile she hoped looked sincere. "The more the merrier, right?" Then she headed up to her room to call Zandra, with Cleo following close behind.

Poolside

Sunday afternoon turned out to be so sunny and hot, it practically had the words *go to the pool* stamped across it. And judging by how crowded it was there, everyone in town must have gotten the message.

Anna Mei and Zandra managed to snag a couple of deck chairs—an older couple was getting up to leave just as the girls were climbing out of the pool. It had been too packed with bodies to swim any actual laps, but they'd had fun jumping in and splashing around.

They'd also spent some time playing with R.J. and Marcus in the smaller pool, the one surrounded by parents and teeming with kids wearing floaties. After a while Mr. and Mrs. Caine had rescued the girls by dragging the younger kids out of the pool and into some shade.

Now they were stretched out in their newly-acquired chairs, towels rolled up under their heads, eyes closed. Anna Mei felt like she could lie there forever, soaking up not only the sun but the sounds and smells, too.

"I think if I had to write a description of summer," she said, her eyes still closed, "it would be about this exact moment—the sunlight reflecting on the water, the smell of coconut lotion mixed with chlorine, everyone laughing and splashing. It would be like a picture of summer but in words."

"Wow, poetic," Zandra said. "But I think my description of summer would be about playing sports—running around outside, getting grass stains on your clothes, and being all sweaty and thirsty until you finally have to go inside for a drink."

Anna Mei laughed. "Not exactly poetic, but I get what you mean. I guess summer can be a lot of different things. There's also the part that's all quiet and peaceful. Like at night, when the stars and the fireflies come out at the same time. Once when Danny and I were—"

She stopped suddenly. The memory she'd been about to describe was a happy one, sharp and clear in her mind. So why had her throat gone dry in the middle of telling Zandra about it?

She opened her eyes and saw that Zandra was looking at her.

"You know," Zandra said, "I've been wondering what's going on with Danny lately. Did you guys have a fight or something?"

A fight? Anna Mei wouldn't exactly call it that. It's not like she and Danny had yelled at each other or slammed doors or anything. It was more like not being sure of him anymore. Like . . . wondering if she even really *knew* him.

But she wasn't sure she wanted to talk about it with Zandra. What if Zandra told her she was making a big deal out of nothing? That would make things worse than before.

"No, no fight," she told Zandra. "It's just that . . . things are different now that we're not in school anymore. We're both busy with other stuff."

"Well, it sure seemed like you were planning to hang out a lot more this summer. And you don't talk about him as much as you used to. I hope everything's okay, that's all. I was wondering if maybe his mom— Hey!"

Zandra sat up suddenly, startled as a couple of boys ran by, shouting and pushing each other. Their wet swimsuits sprinkled the girls with water, and one of them bumped into Zandra's chair before practically falling in her lap.

"Watch it!" she called after them, sitting up to wipe her legs with a towel.

"Looks like the lifeguard's got a hold of them," Anna Mei reported. "And he's handing them over to a girl who—" She stopped, squinting harder in the direction the boys had gone. "Wait a minute, is that . . . Amber?"

Chapter Seventeen

Free Amber

Zandra turned to look at the girl in the bright orange swimsuit and pink sunglasses, who, along with the boys, seemed to be getting a lecture from the lifeguard. "Yep, it's her, all right," Zandra said. "Ponytail and all. She just looks different because she's not attached to Zoey."

That made Anna Mei laugh. Everyone knew that Zoey was the undisputed leader of the Ponytail Club. During the three months that Anna Mei had been a member, Rachel and Amber never challenged Zoey's authority. They seemed to accept that no matter what ideas they came up with, hers would always be better, just by virtue of her complete and utter . . . Zoeyness.

"Those are her brothers—I recognize them now,"

Anna Mei said. "Whenever the club met at her house, she was always telling them to get lost."

Now the lifeguard was gesturing toward her and Zandra. Amber and the two boys all turned to look.

"Heads up," Zandra said. "Here they come."

This time the boys approached slowly, looking like they'd rather be walking the plank. But with Amber practically pushing them from behind, their only choice was to keep going until they reached Zandra's chair.

"Apparently these little monsters have been acting up again," Amber said, over the boys' heads, "and now they have something they want to say to you."

The older boy, his eyes never leaving the ground, mumbled something Anna Mei couldn't quite hear. But a couple of words did sound like "running" and "sorry."

"Yeah," the younger boy said, his voice louder and sounding a little more sincere. "We didn't mean to. We just tripped."

"They've promised not to run anymore or fall on people, right?" Amber demanded, her tone stern, her hands on her hips. Anna Mei figured she probably got a lot of practice using that particular stance. "Or you won't see this pool again until you're both thirty. Got it?"

The boys assured her that they did, and under the watchful eyes of both the lifeguard and their older sister, they slunk off toward the shallow end of the pool and slid meekly into the water.

Amber sighed and turned back to Zandra and Anna Mei. "My dad brought us here, but he needed to take a phone call and asked me to watch them for a few minutes. I should get combat pay."

Zandra smiled. "I know just what you mean," she said. "I have little brothers, too."

"Yeah, I saw them at graduation," Amber said. "So, what have you guys been up to since then? I can't believe it's August already."

Anna Mei was surprised. All three Ponytail girls had more or less avoided her ever since she'd left the club last November. There hadn't been a big scene or anything, just Anna Mei explaining that she didn't feel like she really fit in with the group, and would be spending her time doing other things instead. But Zoey had been icy cold to her ever since, which meant that Rachel and Amber had frozen her out, too.

Now Zandra was telling Amber about their week at volleyball camp, and Amber actually seemed interested.

"I was thinking I might go out for a sport next year," Amber said. "I used to play soccer but I got sort of bored with it after a while. And according to my parents, I won't be getting a horse anytime soon, either. Volleyball sounds like it might be fun."

"It is," Anna Mei heard herself saying. "You

should try it, Amber. Maybe we'll all end up on the same team together."

Amber tilted her head down and looked over the top of her sunglasses at Anna Mei. She seemed to hesitate for a moment, but then she flashed a bright smile and said, "Okay, I'll think about it."

The smile was startling, and not just because it was aimed at Anna Mei. Amber had worn neon green braces all through sixth grade. Like Zandra, she was a natural born smiler, so Anna Mei was used to seeing them a lot. Only now she *didn't* see them.

"Your braces!" she said.

"Yeah, I got them off a few weeks ago," Amber said, "*finally*. I thought I'd never be able to eat popcorn again."

"Well, you look great," Zandra told her.

"Thanks," Amber said, smiling again and proving the point. "Okay, see you guys later."

They watched her head back to the other end of the pool, where her brothers appeared to be taking turns sinking a plastic shark and then retrieving it.

"Huh," Anna Mei said. It wasn't eloquent, but she was at a loss to adequately express her surprise over what had just happened.

"I know, right?" Zandra said, seeming to agree with whatever Anna Mei hadn't been able to put into words. "Maybe that's the real Amber, but Zoey exerts some kind of sinister power over her when they're together. We should start a *Free Amber* campaign."

"Great idea. I'll print up the flyers and you get some buttons made," Anna Mei said, and they both laughed.

It *was* funny, Anna Mei thought, lying back in her chair again. And funny how sometimes, people you thought you knew could do something that made you realize—you didn't really know them at all.

Chapter Eighteen

Kidnapped

On Wednesday, Mrs. Caine dropped Anna Mei off at her house early in the evening.

"Mom? Dad?" Anna Mei called, coming in through the side door.

She expected to find one or both of them in the kitchen, chopping vegetables, stirring a sauce, or doing any of the things they normally did at dinner time. But the kitchen was empty. Nothing simmered on the stove and no warm smells drifted from the oven. Everything was quiet except for the soft ticking of the red clock on the wall.

Anna Mei was about to head upstairs when she heard her mother call, "I'm out here!"

She found her on the patio, sipping lemonade and reading a magazine. Anna Mei thought that with her dark sunglasses, her blond hair spilling out from under a wide-brimmed hat, and her long, tan legs stretched out on the lounge chair, her mother could have posed for a magazine herself.

"For a minute there I thought no one was home," Anna Mei said, plopping down in a chair beside her.

"Just me," Mom said. "Your dad is working late. Did you have a good time at Zandra's?"

Anna Mei smiled, remembering. She and Zandra had spent the afternoon setting up a homemade obstacle course in the Caines' backyard. They'd given R.J. a stopwatch and told him he could be the official timekeeper. Whenever he yelled go, one of the kids would dash through the course—clambering up the ladder, sliding down the slide, tossing whiffle balls into a laundry basket, squeezing under a broom stretched between two chairs, even trundling a wheelbarrow full of garden tools around the yard and across a finish line.

They had all clapped and cheered for each other as they tried to beat their own best times. Finally Mrs. Caine had joined in, first running the course with Marcus riding piggy-back, and then making Zandra raise the broom so she could show them what she called a "proper limbo." When they'd all practically collapsed from exhaustion, she brought out a box of cherry popsicles and herded everyone into the shade to cool off.

"Yeah, it was really fun," Anna Mei said. "It's so

different having a bunch of kids around all the time. There's always something to do."

Mom didn't answer at first. She might have still been looking at her magazine—Anna Mei couldn't tell because of the sunglasses. Finally Mom said, "It does get pretty quiet around here sometimes."

Her voice sounded a little funny, almost as if she were talking to herself instead of to Anna Mei.

"Well," Anna Mei said, "it's definitely quieter without Dad. Are we waiting to have dinner when he gets here?"

"No, he's going to be a while. I don't really feel like cooking, though. I think we should go out for dinner, just the two of us."

Anna Mei looked down at her popsicle-stained shorts and grass-stained knees. She was in no condition to go anywhere. Besides, she was looking forward to just watching some TV tonight, maybe while she chatted online with Lauren. Sometimes they did that while they were watching the same show.

"Actually, I'm kind of a mess," she said. "And I'm pretty tired, too. Why don't we just have frozen dinners instead? Or order in some pizza?"

She expected her mother to shrug and say, "Fine with me." Instead Mom put the magazine down, took her sunglasses off and looked directly into Anna Mei's eyes.

"Go inside and get cleaned up," she said. "You and I are going out for dinner."

Her voice and her look both said, *I'm not kidding.*

Anna Mei blinked in surprise. What could this be about? She'd been gone all day, so whatever it was couldn't be her fault. Maybe Mom was upset about Dad having to work late. Or maybe it was about the trip to Boston. *That* certainly wasn't Anna Mei's fault, either—her parents had been the ones to pull the plug on those plans.

Well, whatever it was, this dinner was obviously going to happen, whether she liked it or not.

"Fine," she said, getting up from the chair. "I'll feed Cleo and then take a quick shower."

Mom put her sunglasses back on and opened her magazine. "See you in a few minutes," she said.

They ended up at a local diner they liked, then both ordered their favorites—a tuna melt for Anna Mei and a turkey sandwich for Mom.

When their drinks came, Mom added a little cream to her coffee and took a sip.

"Mmmm," she said, taking a bigger sip this time. "Diners always seem to have the best coffee. I wonder why that is."

Anna Mei didn't know. She couldn't imagine drinking that stuff at all, although she did like the way it smelled. Somehow it always gave her a warm, cozy feeling that made her think of home. Although right now, she wouldn't exactly call things between her and her mother *cozy*. Something was definitely bugging Mom—she'd barely talked at all on the drive over.

"I know you didn't really want to come with me tonight," Mom said now, as though she'd been reading Anna Mei's thoughts, "but I thought it was important for us to get away from some of the . . . well, *distractions* at home."

Anna Mei looked up from the root beer she'd been sipping. "Like what?"

"Oh, you know—the phone, the computer, TV, even books. It can be pretty hard to have a conversation with you sometimes."

"Come on, Mom, we talk all the time."

"You think so?" Mom sounded genuinely surprised. "I feel like I've barely seen you all summer."

The server brought their food then, which was good timing—it gave Anna Mei a minute to think about what she wanted to say. She reached for the ketchup and squirted some on her plate, next to the fries.

"Okay, I know I've been busy with Zandra lately," she said, "but that's only because we got to know each other so well at camp. Hanging out with her is really fun."

Mom picked up her fork. "Right," she said. "Sort of the way hanging out with Danny used to be fun?"

The bite of tuna Anna Mei had just swallowed seemed to stick in her throat. She grabbed her glass and took a big sip, trying to wash it down. But Mom wasn't waiting for an answer anyway.

"Did you think I wouldn't notice?" she asked. "Danny was at our house practically every day for a while there."

"Exactly," Anna Mei said. Mom had gotten that part right, anyway. "Always at *our* house."

"So why doesn't he come over anymore? Has he done something to upset you?"

Her mother's questions made her feel like she needed to defend herself somehow, and for a moment, she thought about denying it. It wouldn't be easy to explain, after all. Like she'd told Zandra, it's not like there had been any drama.

On the other hand, it might feel good to confide in someone who was bound to understand and to sympathize. Mom might even be willing to talk to Danny herself. If *she* could get Danny to see how unfair he was being, that would sure take some of the pressure off.

Okay then. She took another sip, then a deep breath. It was time to talk about Danny.

Chapter Nineteen

Clearing the Air

She found it hard to stay focused at first, with all the other customers coming and going, and the server stopping by to bring drink refills and desserts. But soon she was telling her mother about what had happened at the nature center and then at Danny's party. Though disappointing, she explained, it was clear to her now that Danny was not the friend she'd thought he was.

Real friendship, she knew, was what she had with Lauren, and what she was building with Zandra. It meant give and take on both sides—you couldn't have one person giving all the time, right? Mom and Dad had told her that practically from birth.

Mom listened while slowly eating her slice of lemon meringue pie. Finally she asked, "So, you're saying Danny isn't living up to your expectations of how a friend should act?"

"Well, yeah, obviously. He wants to hang out at our house all the time—eating with us, playing video games, watching movies. But he's never once invited me over to his house. It's like I'm not good enough to meet his family or something."

"Or something," Mom repeated, laying her fork down on her plate and pushing it aside.

Anna Mei frowned. She was starting to feel a little frustrated at the way this was going. Where was all the support she had expected to get by confiding in her mother?

"What exactly does *that* mean?" she asked.

"It means that you seem to be making this all about you, Anna Mei. *You* feel hurt, *you* feel left out, *you* feel taken advantage of. Now tell me how Danny feels."

"That's just it—I don't know how he feels. We never talk about it."

"So you really have no idea what his reasons are for not introducing you to his family. Don't you think a true friend would try to find out? Maybe you're the one who needs to be putting in more effort."

Anna Mei's frustration was starting to feel more like anger. Not only was Mom *not* sympathizing, she was actually taking Danny's side.

"I don't see how you can say that," she said. "At least I've been trying with Danny—he's the one who keeps pushing me away. Maybe you just don't understand how it feels when someone you care about does that."

At first her mother didn't answer. She kept her eyes fixed on something that seemed to be past Anna Mei's shoulder and outside the window. But when their eyes met again, Anna Mei saw that *this is serious* look on Mom's face, the same one she'd had earlier when she'd insisted on them going out for dinner.

"Believe me, Anna Mei," she said, in a voice that matched the look. "I know *exactly* what that feels like."

Anna Mei stared at her for a moment, trying to make sense of this. She had expected her mother to be concerned about Danny's behavior, but Mom actually sounded hurt by it. Why would she—?

When the realization hit her, the anger that had been bubbling up inside seemed to turn into a cold, hard lump of ice in her chest: *She means me*.

She felt her eyes start to sting, remembering how her mother had tried to make plans for the two of them this summer, over and over again. All of Anna Mei's excuses had made sense when she'd given them, but now they just seemed lame.

"Mom, I didn't . . . I never meant to hurt your feelings," she said, forcing the words past the lump in her throat. "I guess I never thought about it that way. I'm really sorry."

"I know," Mom said, her face and eyes softening

again. "And that's the point I'm trying to make about Danny. I wasn't happy about how you were acting toward me, but I knew you weren't being intentionally cruel or malicious. Just a little . . . thoughtless."

Suddenly everything seemed to click into place. Why hadn't she seen it before? All she needed to do was tell Danny the same thing—get him to see that his behavior was the problem. Once he understood that, he would make her feel better about everything, and things could go back to the way they used to be.

The server stopped by the table with their bill. "Do you ladies need anything else?" he asked, picking up their empty plates.

Mom looked at Anna Mei and smiled. "No, thanks, "she said. "I think we're all set now."

The drive home felt completely different than the one they had taken on the way to the diner. Everything seemed washed clean somehow, as if a giant brush had come and wiped away everything but the slowly-darkening sky, and the low clouds turning pink in the dusky light.

"I'm really glad you made me go tonight," Anna Mei said, as they turned onto their street.

"Well, that's not something a mother hears every day," Mom said. "But I'm glad, too. It was time for us to clear the air."

"I promise I won't make you kidnap me next time," Anna Mei said. "It might not seem like it lately, but I really do like doing stuff together."

"I'm glad," Mom said. "And listen, I know that part of the problem is my work schedule. I'm gone three nights a week, which isn't always good for family time. I'll have to try and see what I can do about that."

The lights were on in the living room when they pulled into their driveway. "Looks like Dad's home," Anna Mei said. "Is it too late for us to watch a movie now?"

"I'm up for it," Mom said, "but your dad's had a pretty long day. It might be just us girls tonight."

Mom parked the car, then reached over and put her arm around Anna Mei's shoulders. "Things will work out with Danny," she said. "And if you get stuck trying to find the right words, well, you can always turn to God for help. Nothing beats prayer for a little inspiration."

Chapter Twenty

Thoughtlessness

Anna Mei had planned to call Danny first thing in the morning. She was anxious to talk to him now, and excited about the idea of finally clearing things up between them. But she slept later than she meant to, partly because she and her mother had stayed up watching the movie, and partly because the sky was dark with rain clouds.

When she finally did punch in his number, it occurred to her that the rain might work in her favor. After all, he couldn't say he was outside painting the house on a day like this, right? Then when he didn't answer at all, she worried that he'd seen her number on caller ID and decided not to pick up.

She ended up leaving a voicemail message about wanting to get together now that she was back from camp. Then she spent a few restless hours trying to distract herself from the whole thing. She ate a late breakfast with her mother, who left for work at noon. She tried curling up in her favorite chair to read for a while, which at least made Cleo happy. But when she found herself having to go back and reread whole paragraphs, she decided it was a lost cause.

"Kind of funny, isn't it, Cleo?" she said, closing the book and setting it on her nightstand. "I kept wishing for a long, rainy day all to myself. But now that I have one, I don't know what to do with it."

Anna Mei went to her dresser and took her notebook from the top drawer. On the very first page she saw the list that she and Danny had made two months ago, at the beginning of summer. Reading it now made her a little sad. But it also made her feel more determined than ever to get things back on track. After all, it was only the beginning of August—there was still time to enjoy summer. They could still do everything on the list.

In fact, she could spend some time online today, doing research for the nature guide project. She could show her work to Danny and get him to do some more illustrations. Then they could start—

When the phone rang she jumped. She could feel her heart pounding, even before she saw that it was Danny's number.

"Hey, you're back," he said. "I thought maybe you and Zandra had decided to quit messing around with amateurs and head straight to the Olympic training village—wherever *that* is."

Anna Mei hadn't known that she'd been holding her breath until she let it out in a long, relieved sigh. He sounded genuinely happy to hear from her. This wasn't going to be so hard after all.

"We thought about it," she said. "But then we decided it wouldn't be fair to deprive Westside Junior High of two such great talents."

She explained that her parents were both working today, so she couldn't leave the house. "But I was hoping we could meet at the nature center tomorrow," she said. "That guide book of ours isn't going to illustrate itself, you know."

"Well, if it did, we'd be rich," he said. "But I can't make it. My dad wants me to work on the shutters so we can finish painting this weekend."

This time Anna Mei's sigh was from frustration instead of relief. It would be hard to wait, but at least he was willing to see her next week. They hung up after making plans for him to come over on Tuesday.

She filled the rest of the day doing research and playing with Cleo. When Dad came home they grilled chicken for dinner. He challenged her to a round of video game basketball, the only kind where being six foot three didn't give him an advantage. He still managed to win, but only by getting lucky enough to make a three-point shot at the buzzer.

Anna Mei thought she'd sleep well now that she'd

connected with Danny again. But lying in bed that night, she felt restless. Even if it wasn't his fault, she was still disappointed that she couldn't see him until Tuesday. After all, she had gotten herself all psyched up to have a serious discussion about his . . . how had Mom described it? His *thoughtlessness*.

She tossed and turned for a while, making a list in her head of the things she planned to say to him. Then she tried to think up possible responses she could make, based on *his* responses. But instead of making her relax, the whole thing started to feel too complicated. It was like trying to solve a math problem that had too many variables—until you knew exactly which ones you were dealing with, you could never get to the right answer.

Finally she remembered what her mother had said about finding inspiration. She cleared her head of all thoughts except a silent prayer that she would find the right words when the time came. It was the last thing she remembered thinking before falling asleep.

At the Front Door

In the morning, Anna Mei woke up knowing that she couldn't spend four more days worrying and wondering. And she wouldn't call first to see if it was okay—she would just ride her bike over to Danny's house and explain that they needed to talk for a few minutes. Then he could get back to his work and she could come home knowing that everything was okay.

She tried to be quiet getting dressed and going downstairs. Her father had already left for the lab, but her mother had worked until midnight and was still sleeping. Anna Mei fed Cleo, then made herself a quick bowl of cereal topped with banana slices. She left a note on the kitchen counter, saying that she'd be back soon and was taking the cell phone in case Mom needed to reach her.

"Wish me luck, Cleo," she said to the cat, who had jumped up onto the kitchen chair the minute Anna Mei got out of it. Cleo's instant meow probably meant *great—a nice warm seat* rather than *good luck*, but it made Anna Mei smile anyway.

She started to go out to the garage for her bike, then came back for the notes she'd made yesterday, just in case. Once they'd worked things out, maybe Danny could take a break from the shutters and they'd end up going to the nature center after all. She was smiling as she headed out the door again.

Danny's neighborhood was older than hers, and closer to the center of town. They had measured the distance once, using the odometer in Dad's car—the two houses were exactly 4.3 miles apart, along mostly suburban roads. It was a pretty easy bike ride, especially on a summer morning when there wasn't much traffic.

But when Anna Mei turned down Danny's street, she was startled at the sight of his house. For some reason she had assumed he and his father and brother were just putting a fresh coat of white over the old paint. Instead the house was now a warm, blue-gray color. Some of the trim still looked worn and faded, but most of it was painted a soft ivory. It really looked great, even with the shutters off.

So Danny hadn't just been making excuses not to see her. He really *had* been busy working on the house. That made her feel even more sure that she was doing the right thing by coming here today. All they needed was to get things out in the open, the way she and her mother had.

She parked her bike in the driveway and walked around to the backyard, in case Danny was painting back there. There was no sign of him or anyone else. Both his parents were probably at work, she figured. And in the summer, a sixteen-year-old like Connor would most likely sleep until noon. She wouldn't risk waking him by ringing the doorbell. She would just open the screen door and knock gently on the—

The front door flew open and someone rushed through it like a freight train, nearly knocking her right off the front step.

"Whoa!" a surprised voice said. A hand reached out to grab her arm before she could fall. "You okay?"

She looked up into a face that was like some weird version of Danny's, as if Danny had been taken over by an older, taller alien. The face wasn't as round as Danny's and not as freckled. It had heavier eyebrows and was topped by darker hair. But it had the same turned up nose and the same blue-green eyes.

Connor.

"I . . . I'm fine," she managed to tell him. "I was wondering if . . . I'm here to see Danny."

She barely got the words out before a car came roaring up into the driveway, windows down and radio blasting. And in case that wasn't quite noisy enough to disturb everyone for miles around, the teenage driver honked his horn twice and yelled, "Come on, Gallagher, let's go!"

"One sec!" Connor answered back. Then turning toward the house he yelled, "Danny! Someone's here for you!"

Anna Mei couldn't hear anything besides the car's engine. But Connor must have, because he called toward the house again, "Yeah, at the front door. Tell Mom I'll be at Drew's house, okay?"

When he turned back toward her she stepped down off the porch, giving him plenty of room to get past her.

"He'll be out in a minute," Connor said. "Sure you're all right?"

Anna Mei nodded, then watched as he practically flew across the grass and leaped into the car. The driver gunned the engine and sped back up the street the same way he'd come. Suddenly everything was still again, with no sound except for a few birds chirping. It had all happened so fast that Anna Mei almost wondered if she had imagined the whole thing.

But it must have been real, because now Danny was at the door. She smiled and was on the verge of joking that she should start calling him "Mini-Connor," but he spoke first.

"What are you doing here?" he asked. "I told you I was busy today."

Turned Away

The harshness in his voice startled her. She felt a hot flush starting to creep up the back of her neck. Suddenly, coming over here without calling first didn't seem like such a good idea.

"I know," she said, deciding to plow ahead anyway. Once she explained things, he would understand why she hadn't wanted to wait. "I just thought if I came over here, it wouldn't take long for us to, you know, talk about things."

Okay, that explanation sounded pretty lame. And even though he was still on the other side of the screen door, she could see that it hadn't done anything to change the look on his face. Then she realized something. Danny wasn't just surprised—he was mad.

"Talk about what," he asked, "volleyball camp? That doesn't exactly seem urgent."

"Well, no . . . but I . . ." She gestured vaguely toward the backpack she'd left sitting by her bike. "I brought my notes for the nature guide. We could talk about that. And . . . well, I thought we should kind of . . . talk about things. Things that have been bothering me lately, I mean. I thought you'd want to know about them."

There. Thank goodness that was over. It hadn't started out the way she'd planned it, but at least now they were getting somewhere. Danny was finally pushing open the screen door and stepping out onto the porch. But then he kept right on going until he was standing, barefoot, next to her bike in the driveway. She seemed to have no choice but to follow him.

He glanced up at one of the upstairs windows, as if expecting to see someone there. His face seemed pale, which was unusual for him. Even his freckles seemed faded somehow.

"Is your dad home?" she asked. "I know he wants you to work today, but maybe it would be okay if I just came in for a minute to—"

"*No*," Danny said, cutting her off. "It's not okay."

Anna Mei stood there, too stunned to even breathe. For the second time today she had the sensation of being with someone who looked like Danny, but wasn't him. Only this time it was worse—much worse.

"Sorry," he said, glancing up at the window again. "I just can't right now." Then he picked up her backpack and handed it to her.

She finally managed to take a ragged breath, but any words she might have wanted to say stayed locked in her throat. She took the backpack from him, then got on her bike and headed down the street, never pausing to look back.

She didn't stop pedaling until she'd gone a couple of miles. Then, panting from exertion and fighting back tears, she made a quick decision to turn onto the road that led to the nature center. Riding along the familiar tree-lined driveway calmed her a little. She was probably a lot safer here, too—in her rush to get away from Danny's house, she'd barely been aware of the cars around her.

The park was already busy this morning. The day camp kids had arrived—she could see them clustered in groups around the education building. But no one was using the bench by the pond, so she walked her bike over there and sat down.

She wouldn't stay long. She just couldn't face going home right now. Her mother would be waiting there, smiling gently and wanting to know how things had gone with Danny. Anna Mei didn't know when she'd be able to talk about it. Right now, *never* seemed like a pretty good guess.

She forced herself to take some deep breaths. A few sips from her water bottle helped, too, although she had to open her backpack to get it, and that meant seeing the folder full of research she'd done on the nature guide project. How could that have only been yesterday? It seemed like a hundred years ago.

It seemed even longer since she'd sat here with Danny, talking and laughing while he sketched and she jotted down observations about wildlife. The first few times had been great. They had talked about how they both loved animals and wouldn't mind being surrounded by them all the time, not just at the nature center.

"We could be like St. Francis," Danny had joked. "You know how all the pictures and statues show him walking around with animals hanging off him?"

Anna Mei had laughed and then told him about a costume party she and Lauren had gone to once, at St. Cecelia's in Boston. The theme was "When the Saints Go Marching In." Lauren and most of the other girls had chosen to dress up like St. Joan of Arc or St. Therese, the Little Flower. But Anna Mei loved the stories about St. Francis of Assisi and the animals—she had wanted to go to the party dressed as him.

"My mom and I found a long, brown robe at the store," she'd told Danny. "It was supposed to be a star fighter Halloween costume, but when we took off the tunic it looked just like a monk's robe. Then she helped me sew some stuffed animals on it, so I had birds on each shoulder, rabbits and squirrels going up the sleeves, even a little curled-up deer attached to the bottom. I could barely move around in that thing, but they said I was the best St. Francis they'd ever seen."

The last time she had been here with Danny, she'd been grouchy from a headache and had questioned him about his mother. That day, he'd been the one to rush off, his mouth set in an angry line, his shoulders hunched over his handlebars.

Now that she thought about it, that was the day everything had started to change between them. But today proved she'd been right all along—he didn't want her at his house or anywhere near his family. That couldn't have been more clear if he'd put a big *KEEP OUT* sign on the lawn, with the words *Anna Mei, This Means You* scrawled underneath.

Shouts and laughter rang out from across the pond, where some of the campers were playing a game of freeze tag with their counselor. Anna Mei closed her eyes, trying to squeeze back the tears that were trying to start again. Her plans to get a job here someday had included Danny. Now she couldn't imagine him in that picture.

She turned her head toward another sound. When she opened her eyes, Danny was there, walking his bike through the grass toward her.

Chapter Twenty-Three

Telling the Truth

It was almost as if her thoughts had conjured him up.

"I was on my way to your house," he said, "but I thought I should check here first, just in case. Guess I know you pretty well, Cartoon Girl."

His smile was a pale ghost of the one she was used to seeing, the one that lit up his whole face. She turned away from it, away from him.

"*Don't*," she said, in a voice that almost hissed. "Don't ever call me that again."

She heard rather than saw him lay his bike down and sit on the grass next to it.

"I'm sorry, Anna Mei," he said, leaving out the forced humor he'd tried before. "I mean, that's what I came to tell you. I'm really sorry about the way I acted at my house. I was just so surprised to see you there."

There was no way to leave without walking past him, and she didn't feel ready to stand up yet anyway. The best she could do was keep her eyes fixed straight ahead and hope he would go away soon.

"It doesn't matter," she said.

"Of course it matters," he said. "You're my friend."

That made her turn toward him, eyes wide. She was sure he'd be smiling, since that had to be another joke. But he was looking down at the ground, not at her.

"Your *friend*?" she said. "How can you say that? Apparently hanging out with me at school is okay, but you practically shoved me out of your yard. I'm not allowed to go to your house, let alone come inside. I don't know about you, but I can't be friends with someone who thinks I'm not even good enough to meet his family."

"Not good enough to . . . ?" he repeated, looking up now. "Is *that* what you think?"

She should have known he would deny it.

"Come on, Danny, at least be honest. You know we always hang out at *my* house, with *my* parents. They've practically adopted you. Meanwhile you've deliberately kept me away from *your* family ever since I've known you. And if you tell me I've been imagining all this I'm getting on that bike and going home right now."

He looked away again, then started to pull random blades of grass out of the ground and twist them together.

"Fine," she said, forcing herself to stand up and take a step toward her bike.

"No, wait," he said, getting to his feet, too. Now he was looking straight into her eyes. "There's something I should have told you a long time ago. Please stay, so I can tell you now."

She was tempted to tell him she wasn't interested. It was hard to imagine any reason he could come up with that would excuse the way he'd been acting toward her.

But that look in his eyes stopped her. He wasn't joking now. In fact, she'd never seen him look so upset before.

"All right," she said, "but just for a few minutes." She thought of her mother, waiting at home. "I just need to call my mom first, so she knows I'll be a little while longer."

Danny stayed on his feet, only now he started pacing back and forth between the pond and the bench. Anna Mei made the call and then sat down again, waiting. Just when she thought he must have changed his mind about the whole thing, he came and stood beside her.

"Okay," he said. "Remember when you first moved here, how worried you were about fitting in at school?"

She frowned. Of course she remembered that—but he was supposed to be explaining *his* problem, not something that had happened almost a year ago.

"You kept doing things you thought would make you seem like everyone else," he went on, apparently intent on revisiting her past instead of getting to the point. "Sometimes you even did things that made other people feel bad—like your parents. And, well . . . me."

The anger she had tried to tamp down was starting to flicker again. Somehow Danny was turning what she thought would be an apology into an accusation. Sure, she had made a few mistakes last year, but once she apologized and made some changes, everyone had moved on. So what was the point of bringing all that up now?

"One of the things you told me back then was that I didn't understand how it felt being different—trying to hide things about yourself so other people wouldn't look at you funny. But the truth is, I *did* know how it feels. I've been trying to hide something, too. And as you've figured out by now, it's about my family."

Well, now they were getting somewhere. But what could be so bad about his family that he had to hide it from *her*? They obviously all lived together in that house, so his parents probably weren't divorced.

And she'd just seen Connor—Danny looked exactly like him. There was no chance of *him* being adopted. Besides, if it was anything like that, he would have just told her.

He seemed to be waiting for her to answer, but all she could think of was the obvious question: "What about them?" she asked.

"They're—I guess I should say *we're*—not like your family," he said. "We don't joke around or hang out together. At least, not anymore."

She felt a prickly sensation on the back of her neck. The way he said "not anymore" made her feel that whatever he was about to say was really important—maybe even the most important thing he'd ever told her.

"Did something . . . happen?" she asked.

Finally Danny sat down next to her. She heard him take a deep breath. "Three years ago, when I was nine," he said, "we found out my mother had cancer."

Chapter Twenty-Four

Blown Apart

It had all started with some swelling in her neck, Danny explained. She thought it was just an infection. But when it didn't go away and her doctor did more tests, their family was stunned to learn that she had lymphoma, a kind of cancer that attacks white blood cells. She started treatment right away. And while Danny understood that none of this was her fault, he couldn't help resenting the sudden changes in his life.

"I remember visiting her in the hospital," he said. "Then I remember her being tired all the time. There were a lot of things she couldn't do anymore. My dad tried to take care of all of us, but he had to go to work. In fact, he had to work as much as he could, in order to pay all the extra bills."

Everyone knew his mother was sick, he said—it wasn't like they were trying to keep it a secret or anything. At first people brought meals over, and her name was added to the prayer list at St. Brigid's. His grandparents came to help out sometimes, and so did the aunts who lived in Indiana. That first summer, they had even taken Danny back there with them. But he'd been so homesick and miserable they'd had to let him go home.

Then as the months went on, people started to act like the whole situation had just blown over. Kids and teachers stopped asking him how his mother was doing. He'd been glad, really. Cancer was a pretty scary thing, and it had already taken over his life at home. At least at school he could pretend that everything was all right.

"Besides, she really was getting better," he said. "The chemotherapy and radiation were the hardest parts, but after that, she started getting stronger again. The doctors said her lymphoma was in remission. It wasn't the same as 'cured', but for a couple of years they kept saying how great she was doing. I started to believe things would get back to the way they were before."

He paused then and she tried to think of something to say, but her mind just didn't seem to be working normally. The words in her head skittered away when she tried to put them together into sentences.

But Danny wasn't finished yet anyway.

"Then about a year ago, just when school was starting," he said, "one of her checkups didn't go so well. She had to go back into the hospital for more tests. We were afraid everything was starting all over again."

It took a while, he went on, but finally all the test results came back and the doctors said everything was fine. Just a false alarm, they called it. Of course Danny's whole family was grateful and relieved, but it made him realize that this could happen again any time, and that maybe things would never really get back to the way they used to be.

He looked out across the pond, where the campers had finished their game and were sitting in a circle, having a snack. For a moment, Anna Mei wished she could join them. Or better yet, *be* one of them—just a six or seven-year-old kid, with nothing to worry about except what flavor of juice box the counselor would give you.

But she knew Danny was waiting for her to say something. And really, there was only one thing she *could* say: "I'm really sorry, Danny." Her voice sounded strange and unnatural to her own ears. "I just . . . didn't know."

"*Of course* you didn't know," he said. "That was the whole point of keeping you away from them. When I was with you, I didn't have to talk about it, or even think about it."

She tried to make sense of this. "But if the doctors

said everything is okay, why is it still so hard to talk about?"

Danny sighed again, a deep sound that seemed to come from way down inside. "I don't know," he said. "I guess because it doesn't *feel* okay. It feels like . . . like a bomb went off and blew a big hole in my family. Since then things haven't been the same for us. My dad still works all the time. We all worry every time my mom gets sick or feels tired, in case it means the cancer is coming back. And Connor . . ."

His voice trailed off and she thought he might just leave it at that. She could see the effort it was taking for him to finish, but he seemed determined to do it.

"It's kind of hard to talk about Connor," he said. "He was thirteen when this all started, so he ended up having to take care of me a lot. For a while we were really close—even in the worst times I could count on him. I realize now how hard that must have been, and how scared he must have felt. After I got older and Mom got better, I guess Connor figured he could finally escape from it all. He spends most of his time with his friends instead of with us."

It was all so much to take in. When she wanted to know what was going on with Danny, she had never imagined something like this. He was—well, he was *supposed* to be—her happy-go-lucky friend, the guy who loved jokes and cartoons and funny movies. This boy sitting next to her, talking about fear and pain and sadness, seemed like a stranger.

She tried again to think of something to say. "I . . . I can see now why you liked being at my house."

"Yeah, I guess I've been doing a little escaping of my own," he admitted. "That very first time I came over, to work on the mold terrarium, remember? My mom was just about to go into the hospital then, to have the tests done. It felt so great to joke around with you and your dad that day. I realized that since you were new here, you didn't know anything about me or my family. I could just relax when I was around you."

As if just realizing how that sounded, he quickly added, "Don't get me wrong—I honestly like all of you, even Emily and Benjy. But part of what I like is just being around people who aren't always tired or worried or upset."

He looked over at her then. "And the food's not bad either," he said, managing a sort of half-smile.

Anna Mei wished she could laugh at that, wished she could meet him halfway so they could get past this strange, awkward moment. But she just didn't have it in her. All she could think about was getting away—not just from him, but from the feeling that everything had been turned upside down.

She reached for her backpack. "Listen, I'm glad you told me," she said. "And if there's anything I can do to . . . you know, *help*, just let me know. But right now I really have to go. My mom's waiting and I—"

She stopped, resisting the urge to smack herself on the forehead. What a stupid thing to do, mentioning her *mother* at a time like this.

"Anyway, I'll call you later, okay? Oh—I wanted to tell you," she said, relieved when a random thought jumped into her head. "You're doing a great job painting the house. I really like that color."

The old Danny would have answered with a joke, like telling her how all the great artists had gotten their start painting houses. But all this Danny did was look at her for a moment, then quietly say, "Thanks. My mom picked it out."

Suddenly Anna Mei realized that the reason he had kept looking up at the window was to see if his mother was standing there. It made her imagine Mrs. Gallagher as one of those pale, shadowy figures in a movie, silently drawing back the curtains to get a glimpse of the world outside.

Anna Mei shivered. Then for the second time that morning, she got on her bike and rode away, leaving Danny behind.

A Big Eraser

The weekend seemed to drag on endlessly. Anna Mei felt restless and bored, searching for ways to fill up her time. It didn't help that Zandra was out of town at a family reunion, and Lauren was away at swim camp. Even Dad was busy with work he'd brought home, still trying to catch up from the Seattle trip.

On Saturday, Aunt Karen came over to help Mom make bread, pies, and cookies for a church bake sale. Anna Mei joined them for a while. Doing ordinary things like measuring flour and cracking eggs in a bowl helped to take her mind off things. But when the kitchen got too hot and the work got too boring, she bailed out.

Besides, every once in a while she caught her

mother looking at her with that expression Anna Mei recognized—the one that meant *I'm worried about you*.

"How did it go?" Mom had asked on Friday, when Anna Mei came home from the nature center. "Did you two get things straightened out?"

Anna Mei had intended to tell her the whole story—all about how Danny had only been pretending that everything was fine, when all the time he'd been keeping this big secret. Worse than that, he'd been coming over to their house to get away from the problems at his own.

But standing there while her mother waited, she couldn't get the words out. A million thoughts and feelings were all jumbled up inside. How would she ever be able to explain things she didn't understand herself?

Finally Anna Mei just said that Danny's mother had been sick, and although she would be fine, she needed time to recover. That's why his parents hadn't been very social lately, and why it wasn't a good idea to have people over right now.

"So you were right, Mom. It really didn't have anything to do with me at all."

"Is there anything we can do to help?" Mom had asked. "I'd be happy to take some meals over there, or even help with medical questions if they have any. Did Danny say what kind of illness it was?"

Talking about it at all had been hard enough—somehow saying the word *cancer* to her mother was more than she could handle.

"He didn't really want to talk about that part," she said, which was true even if it left out a few details. "I mean, his mom is better now, and that's all that matters, right? I'll ask him about the food, though."

She would have liked to make a joke about the low odds of Danny turning down an offer of food, but she was afraid the words would stick in her throat. Instead she made an excuse about needing a shower after her long bike ride, then scooted away.

Sunday was no better. There'd been an especially rough moment at Mass, when *The Prayer of St. Francis* was announced as the closing hymn. The words of that song sent Anna Mei back to the beginning of summer, laughing with Danny over the story of her animal-encrusted costume.

Everything was so simple then, she thought. *Why didn't I just leave it alone?*

Now she wished she could take a big eraser and make last Friday disappear the way Danny got rid of things in his sketches he didn't like. Sometimes he tore out a whole page and just crumpled it up—then like magic, that scene was gone forever. Doing that in real life would mean she'd never have gone over to his house, never confronted him or found out his secret. Everything would be the way it was before. Only this time she wouldn't care if they were always at her house or if she never met his parents—what did that matter, anyway?

But it was too late. She knew Danny's secret now, and things would never be the same again.

Thankfully, the Caines came home from their reunion on Sunday evening. By bedtime the girls were making plans for Anna Mei to spend the next day at Zandra's, and then sleep over until Tuesday. She had already made plans with Danny for Tuesday, but that was before . . . everything. He'd probably forgotten all about it anyway.

"All right," Mom said, when Anna Mei ran the idea past her. "I can drop you off on my way to work."

"But that's not until noon," Anna Mei pointed out. "Can you take me, Dad? Then I could be there all morning, too."

"Wow, if you're willing to get up at eight o'clock in the morning during summer vacation, you girls must have something really special lined up," he said.

But they didn't—that was the great thing about going to Zandra's. It was easy to get lost in the shuffle, to disappear into the good-natured chaos of life at the Caine house. You never had to be alone with just your thoughts.

Even dinnertime there seemed like an adventure, with everyone talking and passing food around while Mrs. Caine kept a watchful eye on things.

"Don't you know I see everything?" she would announce, even if she was at the stove with her back turned. “Aleesha, those carrots you just hid under the potatoes better find a way into your stomach, or that ice cream I bought today is going to stay nice and cozy, right there in the freezer.” And everyone at the table would erupt with laughter—except for Aleesha, who’d sigh and then eat the potatoes, carrots and all.

Chapter Twenty-Six

Not So Simple

Anna Mei was looking forward to finding a similar scene at breakfast when her father dropped her off on Tuesday morning. But when Mrs. Caine answered the door and led her into the kitchen, only Marcus sat at the table, still wearing his pajamas.

"Zandra will be down in a few minutes," Mrs. Caine said. "She was in the shower last time I checked. And Aleesha's sleeping in. I guess we're all a little tired after our busy weekend."

"What about R.J.?" Anna Mei asked, missing the sweet, welcoming smile he always had for her. "Is he sleeping, too?"

Mrs. Caine shook some cereal into Marcus's bowl, then added milk. "No, not sleeping," she said. "But he isn't ready to come down just yet. He's having breakfast in his room."

"Is something wrong?" Anna Mei asked. She hoped R.J. wouldn't have to miss all the fun today.

"Not really," Mrs. Caine said. She took a long knife from the drawer and started slicing into a cantaloupe. "It's just that R.J. is the kind of child who likes to have his own things around him. He likes his routine. Any time we have to go away or be around new people, he gets kind of . . . upset. It takes him a few days to settle down again."

Anna Mei watched Mrs. Caine chop the melon into juicy chunks. She always seemed to have the situation under control, no matter what it was. Zandra was like that, too. No one in this family fell apart just because one of them didn't feel well.

"R.J. was crying at Uncle Robert's house," Marcus reported. "He's a scaredy cat sometimes."

When Zandra came into the kitchen a few minutes later, Mrs. Caine was giving Marcus a stern lecture about name calling and brotherly love. She sent him upstairs to get dressed and then went to check on R.J., so the two girls ended up eating breakfast alone at the big table.

The rest of the morning didn't exactly go the way Anna Mei had planned, either. The kickball game she suggested never got off the ground. No one wanted to build another obstacle course. Aleesha was mad at Zandra over something that had happened at the reunion—Anna Mei never did quite get the whole story. Marcus was sulking because Aleesha wouldn't let him play her new video game. And by lunch time, R.J. still hadn't come out of his room.

"I swear I've never seen a more ornery bunch of kids in my life," Mrs. Caine said, fixing a peanut butter and jelly sandwich to take to him.

Hearing that word made Anna Mei remember her Grandmother Anna. She had died a few years ago, but she was the only other person Anna Mei ever knew who said "ornery." When she was little, it used to make her picture a herd of grouchy billy goats in a field, butting their heads together.

"Sorry, Mom," Zandra said. She'd been loading lunch dishes into the dishwasher, but now she paused to give her mother a hug. "We'll straighten up, I promise."

"I should hope so," Mrs. Caine said. "I'm counting on you and Anna Mei to hold down the fort while I take Aleesha to her eye doctor appointment. I just don't think R.J. is up to coming with me, and Marcus is busy playing with his trucks in the sandbox. I'll be back in about an hour, all right?"

After she and Aleesha had gone, Zandra and Anna Mei stayed in the kitchen, where they could see Marcus from the window.

"I guess we *have* been pretty grouchy today," Zandra said. "You probably wish you'd stayed home, or gone over to Danny's instead."

An image of Danny standing in his driveway, holding out her backpack, flashed into Anna Mei's mind. For a moment she considered telling Zandra the whole story, but she wasn't sure that was fair to Danny. He'd made it clear that the less his friends knew about the situation, the better.

Besides, she'd come over here today to forget all that. "Well, you know what they say—even a grouchy Caine is . . . uh, better than no Caine," she finished lamely.

"Somehow I doubt you read that in Confucius or Aesop," Zandra said.

"Nope—a fortune cookie. Of course, I got it from O'Leary's Discount Chinese Take-out, so . . ." She shrugged to show that her source might be a little less than trustworthy.

Zandra laughed, then said that Anna Mei had given her an idea. "Let's make some of those peanut butter cookies R.J. likes. Maybe it will cheer him up."

"Are you sure your mom won't mind?"

"We'll just mix up the dough," Zandra said. "We won't turn on the oven until she gets back. You get the eggs and butter from the fridge while I find the recipe, okay?"

As they got busy collecting the ingredients, Anna Mei decided to ask Zandra something she'd been wondering about. "This thing R.J. has," she said, "his autism. I don't really understand what it is."

Zandra spooned some peanut butter out of the jar and into a measuring cup. "That's just it," she said, "no one does. They're not sure what causes it, or why it happens more with boys than girls. But we all knew something was different about R.J., even when he was a baby. He didn't like to be touched and held the way babies usually do. He could cry for hours after hearing a loud noise or being startled by something. And once he picked out his favorite blanket and stuffed animal, he could never calm down or go to sleep without them. He still can't."

"Will he ever grow out of it?" Anna Mei asked. It made her sad to think of sweet little R.J., always struggling to make sense of things.

Zandra shook her head. "No, it doesn't work like that. He'll always see and feel the world differently than most people. But he's a really smart kid, and he can learn to cope. In fact, that's what a lot of his therapy is about—learning ways to break things down into smaller chunks so he can handle them. Right now we're doing a lot of that for him, like showing him pictures to help him remember things, or telling him in advance what's going to happen, or trying not to change anything too much or too suddenly."

"That must be kind of hard," Anna Mei said, realizing that things might not be quite as simple at the Caine house as she'd thought. "I mean, having to sort of tiptoe around all the time, trying not to upset him."

Zandra dumped some sugar into the mixing bowl, her face thoughtful. "It is sometimes. It would be a lot easier if R.J. was more like everyone else. But then he wouldn't be—"

She stopped suddenly, distracted by a glance out the window. "Now where has Marcus disappeared to?" she said. "He knows he's not allowed to leave the yard."

"I'll go find him," Anna Mei said, rinsing her hands at the kitchen sink. "He's probably just—"

Her words were cut off by the sound of a loud scream, followed by a sickening crash.

Chapter Twenty-Seven

Things Get Messy

For a moment the girls stood frozen in shock, looking at each other. Then they both rushed in the direction of the noise—the door that led from the kitchen to the garage.

They found Marcus lying on the floor, clutching a plastic watering can to his chest and sobbing uncontrollably. Trowels, seed packets, planter trays, sprayer heads, and garden stakes lay scattered around him. A bag of potting soil had split open, spilling rich, black dirt across the garage floor. On top of the whole mess lay a long, wooden shelf, partially covering Marcus.

"What happened?" Zandra cried, pushing away the shelf and then kneeling beside her brother.

Marcus loosened his death grip on the watering

can so he could hold onto Zandra instead. "I'm s-s-sorry, Zannie!" he cried, his voice muffled against her shoulder. "I didn't mean to—it just b-b-broke!"

"Are you all right?" she asked, trying to pry him away so she could check him over. "Did you hit your head?"

"No," Marcus answered in a choking voice that sounded as miserable as he looked. "Just my arm and my leg. See?" He twisted and turned to show her, moving both limbs easily.

"Oh, Marcus," she said, wiping his dirty, tear-stained face with his shirt. "Were you trying to climb up those shelves?"

Anna Mei could see now what must have happened. A shelf just a few feet above the garage floor was still attached by brackets to the wall. Marcus must have been standing on that one and holding onto the shelf above it, trying to reach the watering can. His weight had pulled the higher shelf off its brackets and brought it crashing down on top of him, along with everything that had been stored on it.

"I just wanted to wash my trucks!" he wailed.

"All right, hush now," Zandra said, getting to her feet and pulling Marcus gently to his. "You're fine, you just scraped your arm right here, see?" She pointed to a raw patch just below his elbow. "It's bleeding a little but that's—"

"No, no, no, no, no!"

The heart-wrenching cry startled Anna Mei. For a split second she was confused—the sound wasn't coming from Marcus. In fact, he was staring wide-eyed at something right behind her, and so was Zandra. Anna Mei turned and saw R.J. standing at the kitchen door, both hands over his ears, his face contorted in a cry of anguish that seemed to go on and on.

"No, no, no, no, no!"

Anna Mei started toward him, instinctively feeling the need to calm him the way Zandra had calmed Marcus. But he stepped back away from her, his screams growing even more frantic, his feet now stomping to their rhythm.

"He won't let you touch him!" Zandra said, raising her voice to be heard. "You take Marcus inside and start cleaning him up. There's antiseptic in the cabinet under the bathroom sink."

Anna Mei might have protested but Zandra was already at R.J.'s side, coaxing him into the house and away from the mess. Marcus watched them go, his lips trembling, the tears spurting again from his big, brown eyes.

"Don't worry, R.J.!" he called after them. "I'm okay! Don't cry!"

Hearing Marcus trying to comfort his brother made Anna Mei feel like bursting into tears herself. But she knew that wouldn't help anyone—especially not Marcus, and he was counting on her now. She took a deep breath to steady herself, then put her arm around his small shoulders.

"Come on," she said. "We need to get you cleaned up and looking all handsome again for when your mom gets home. I'll bet she'll be so proud of the way you and Zandra took care of R.J. while she was gone."

Marcus sniffled and wiped his nose with his shirt sleeve. "She will?"

"Of course," Anna Mei answered. "You're a really great brother, Marcus."

The tiny smile she got in return gave her the courage to keep going, one foot in front of the other, right through the kitchen door and on into the house.

When Mrs. Caine arrived about ten minutes later, Anna Mei could honestly say she'd never been so happy to see someone in her whole life. She felt completely unprepared for this scenario—one that had put her in charge of a little boy with blood on his arm and anguish in his eyes.

Once Mrs. Caine knew Marcus was all right, she took him upstairs with her to check on R.J. A few minutes later, Zandra came down and reported that R.J. had started to calm down once he'd seen that his little brother was fine.

"It was a big help having you here," she told Anna Mei. "It would have been a lot harder without you."

Zandra still wanted her to stay for dinner and the sleepover, but Anna Mei couldn't imagine doing that now. All she could think about was getting home, where no one needed her except Cleo, and she could just be by herself in the peace and quiet.

Chapter Twenty-Eight

Peace and Quiet

"I'm not feeling that great myself," Anna Mei told Zandra. "I think we should try the sleepover again next week."

She didn't want to ask Mrs. Caine for a ride home, but she didn't want to wait until her father got off work, either. When she called him and explained what had happened, he agreed to come over on his lunch hour and pick her up.

Back at their house, he waited while she took a long, hot shower.

"I've got your shirt soaking in the laundry tub," he said, when she came downstairs again. "That blood stain should come out in cold water, if the instructions on the detergent box haven't steered me wrong. Are you sure you don't want something to eat?"

Anna Mei shook her head. "No, I'm not hungry. You should go back to work, Dad. I'll be fine."

"I know you will," he said, putting his arm around her shoulders. "I'm very proud of you, you know. It sounds like you and Zandra had a few scary moments there, but you handled it great."

"It was mostly Zandra," Anna Mei said. "She's good at handling things."

"Thank goodness," Dad said. "All right, I'll go for a few hours but I'll be back around five-thirty, okay? You just relax and enjoy the peace and quiet."

It wasn't until he was gone and she looked around the empty house that she heard his words echoing in her head. *Peace and quiet.* It was what she longed for when she'd wanted to come home. But wasn't it also exactly what she'd been avoiding by going to Zandra's in the first place?

She flopped down on the couch, feeling suddenly exhausted by what had happened—and not just today. Cleo jumped up immediately, claiming her favorite spot on Anna Mei's lap.

"How did everything get to be such a mess, Cleo?" she asked, stroking the cat's head and back. "All I wanted was to have a nice, relaxing summer with my friends. The next thing I know I'm rushing off to Danny's to try and fix things with him, then rushing home to get away from him. Then I decide it's too quiet at home so I rush off to Zandra's where nothing is ever quiet. What in the world am I *doing*?"

A word jumped into her head, one that Danny had used just a few days ago: *Escaping*.

He had said it first about Connor, who had found a way to avoid his burdens by taking off with his friends. Then he'd said it about himself, describing how he had found refuge from his fear and anger by being with her family instead of his own.

Hearing that had made her mad. It felt as though Danny had just been using their friendship to smooth over the rough patches in his own life. But wasn't she doing exactly the same thing every time she went running off to Zandra's?

Ever since that weekend before volleyball camp, she'd been thinking of the Caines' house as a place to escape from her problems. She had treated it like going to a real circus, where all the crowds and commotion were noisy enough to drown out everything else.

But that had been an illusion, she realized now. The Caines were real people who had real problems of their own. Only instead of trying to run away, like she was, they were dealing with their problems as best they could. Even when it was hard, they never stopped trying to help R.J. learn—what had Zandra said?—how to cope. R.J. could always count on them.

Last year, when Anna Mei was struggling to find a way to fit in, she'd had someone to count on, too. Danny had helped her solve her problem by encouraging her to be honest about who she really was.

But what had *she* done when he was the one with a problem?

She felt a sudden flush burning her neck and face. All this time Anna Mei had been telling herself that Danny was the one letting their friendship down—letting *her* down. And all this time she'd been exactly wrong.

"We'd better go upstairs and get my notebook, Cleo," she said, gathering the cat in her arms and getting to her feet. "I think I'm going to need a whole different kind of list."

Chapter Twenty-Nine

Somebody's Strength

"Oh my goodness, what's all this?" Mom asked, propping a pillow behind her so she could sit up in bed. She had worked past midnight, so was just waking up at nine-thirty.

Anna Mei was standing in the doorway with a tray of food. "Well, I figured out that I owe you roughly four thousand breakfasts," she said, setting the tray down on the nightstand next to the bed. "I thought it was time I started paying you back."

The whole breakfast-in-bed thing was actually part of her new plan, the one she'd come up with yesterday and labeled *Things to Do—Better*. One of the things she had put at the top of the list was "Spend time with Mom." In fact, she'd written it in all caps and added three exclamation points. Breakfast today had seemed as good a place to start as any.

"I don't know how to use the coffee maker," she said. "But there's orange juice, and fruit, and I toasted the bagel the way you like it, light on the cream cheese."

Mom smiled as she picked up a napkin, then a bowl of sliced peaches. "It's just lovely, Anna Mei. I hope you're going to join me."

"Actually, I already ate a while ago. I didn't really . . ." She hesitated for a moment, then took a breath and plowed on. "I didn't sleep very well last night."

Her mother reached over and patted the bed next to her. "Come on," she said. "Maybe it will help to talk about it. Are you still upset about what happened yesterday at Zandra's?"

"Well, not exactly," Anna Mei said. She climbed into the bed, drawing her knees up and cradling a pillow in her lap. "I called Zandra last night and she said the boys are both fine. R.J. settled down after a while, and Marcus just has a couple of bruises and a bandage—he didn't need stitches or anything."

"That's good news," Mom said, taking a sip of juice. "A lot of people who come to the emergency room are injured at home. Kids Marcus's age need to be watched every minute."

"That's what Mrs. Caine said, too. Zandra and I thought we *were* being careful. I guess sometimes, even if you don't mean for someone to get hurt, it can happen anyway."

Something in Anna Mei's voice must have given her away, because her mother stopped eating and said gently, "Somehow I get the feeling we're not talking about Marcus anymore."

Anna Mei nodded. "It's . . . it's about Danny. I really need some help figuring out what to do, Mom."

"Well, as you said, people can hurt each other without meaning to. Didn't he explain that his problems were about his family situation and not you?"

"Yes, only . . . I'm not talking about the way Danny's been treating me," she said. "I'm talking about the way I've been treating *him*."

Little by little, the story spilled out. She told her mother how serious Mrs. Gallagher's illness really was, and how Danny had tried to hide it from her so he could feel happy and safe again. Then once she'd pushed him into finally telling her about it, she had tried to run away from the whole thing. She felt awful about it, but now the hole she was in seemed too deep. How would she ever be able to dig herself out?

"Maybe you're being a little hard on yourself," Mom suggested. "After all, Danny's family has had years to learn how to live with the situation. It's all new for you. It's no wonder you're feeling overwhelmed."

Anna Mei felt that same rush of shame that had come over her yesterday. "But as soon as he told me, I wanted it all just to go away. I wanted everything to be like it was before. I wanted Danny to be like *he* was before, too."

"But you thought your friendship was simple and uncomplicated. He *wanted* you to think that. Finding out that he's been dealing with some serious problems is bound to change things."

Anna Mei sighed and leaned over to rest her head against her mother's shoulder. She'd come this far—she might as well get it all out.

"I think . . . it's not just what's happened between Danny and me," she said, noticing the trembling in her voice but unable to stop it. "It's that . . . the whole thing scares me. If Danny's mom can get a disease like this, then so can anyone. So can . . . you."

"I know," Mom said gently, reaching up to smooth Anna Mei's hair. "People at the hospital get bad news sometimes, and they're scared. I think it's natural to feel that way. We like to be in control of things—certainly of ourselves. And sometimes we're just not. We have to accept that."

"But isn't it hard for you? I mean, to be around people who are sick and might. . ." she swallowed hard, "might never get better?"

"Sometimes," her mother said. She leaned over, opened the drawer of her nightstand and pulled out a book. "I have a favorite poem that helps me when that happens. It reminds me that we're not in this alone."

She flipped through the pages until she found the right one, then started to read aloud:

For God hath not promised skies always blue,
Flower-strewn pathways all our lives through;
God hath not promised sun without rain,
Joy without sorrow, peace without pain.

But God hath promised strength for the day,
Rest for the labor, light for the way,
Grace for the trials, help from above,
Unfailing sympathy, undying love.

She left the book in her lap and pulled Anna Mei close again. "Sometimes," she said, "the best you can do is try to be somebody's 'strength for the day.' The rest is in God's hands."

Anna Mei sighed. She could feel the ball of fear and confusion that had knotted her stomach starting to relax a little. "Danny was supposed to come over here today," she said. "I'm going to call him and see if he still wants to. I wouldn't blame him if he said no, after the way I've acted."

"Do you want me to ask him?" Mom asked. "I could invite him over for dinner."

Another time that would have made Anna Mei smile. This time she felt her eyes well up with tears, remembering all the fun mealtimes Danny and her family had shared. It would be terrible if they never had a chance to do that again.

"Thanks, Mom, but I think I need to do this

myself. Maybe I can even be Danny's 'strength' for today."

Her mother kissed the top of her head, and they stayed like that, side by side, for just a little while longer.

Chapter Thirty

A Package Deal

Riding her bike along the path at the nature center, Anna Mei had a strange sensation that everything happening at this moment had already happened before.

If this were a book or a movie, she might actually be repeating the same day over again. But this was real life, and she just needed to shake the feeling off. Besides, there were plenty of differences between that terrible day and now.

For one thing, she wasn't trying to get away from Danny this time. In fact, she was anxious to see him. Although he had turned down her invitation for dinner, he had agreed to meet her here. It was a start anyway.

The weather wasn't as nice as it had been last week, either. The long stretch of hot, sunny days had ended, and today the sun was hidden behind a thick cover of clouds.

Once she got near the pond she noticed another difference—a new bird feeding station had been installed at the water's edge. Judging by how crowded it was, it hadn't taken the birds long to discover it. Most were sparrows and finches. A pair of red birds arrived together, then a bluejay bullied his way in.

There were a few species she didn't recognize, though. She wished she'd brought her notebook so she could describe them and look them up later. That was another difference—she'd had her notebook with her before, planning to impress Danny with all the work she'd done.

In fact, pretty much everything she'd done that day had been about her. She'd gone to his house to talk about her hurt feelings. She'd felt sorry for herself when, instead of apologizing, he had shared his own problems. Then she'd spent the rest of the time wishing she could have the old, carefree Danny back.

Now, watching the birds and hearing their happy chatter, she thought of St. Francis again. She remembered how he had prayed for an understanding heart: "Grant that I may not so much seek to be consoled as to console, to be understood as to understand, to be loved as to love."

I've had it all backwards, Anna Mei thought. *I just hope it's not too late to make it right again.*

When Danny came riding up the path a few minutes later, she had to smile. He was wearing the *Anime Rules* shirt she had given him for his birthday—that must be a good sign, right?

"Hi," she said, as he parked his bike next to hers. "Did your dad let you off for good behavior, or did you finally get the painting done?"

"It's done," he said. "And it wasn't all bad—I actually liked spending some time with my dad and Connor. But I sincerely hope to never see another can of paint as long as I live. At least not one that has *Oceanside Blue* in it."

"Well, you did a really good job on the house."

He looked down at the grass, then over at the pond. "Thanks, but actually . . . I was thinking that I didn't give you much of a chance to see it the other day."

It was the perfect opening, and she grabbed it. "That's what I wanted to talk to you about," she said. "I didn't handle things very well that day, Danny. I wanted you to know that I'm sorry."

He turned and looked at her. "Listen, I'm the last person who knows the right way to handle things," he said. "I've pretty much done everything wrong from the beginning."

It wasn't the answer she'd expected. "What do you mean?"

"You know—the whole keeping-it-all-a-secret

thing. As if pretending my mom's cancer didn't exist would somehow make it go away."

"Well, you were just a kid when it all started," she reminded him.

"I know, and maybe it's okay for a kid to act that way. But here I am three years later, still keeping my friends away from her and telling myself it's so she can rest, or so she won't catch a cold or something."

"But isn't that true?"

"It started out that way, but the real reason isn't her—it's me. It's not that I think having cancer is something to be ashamed of—I just didn't want to have to talk about it, or even think about it. And I definitely didn't want people treating me differently because of it."

Anna Mei smiled at that—she couldn't help it. "Danny, look who you're talking to! I practically invented the *I-don't-want-people-to-treat-me-differently* thing. You were the one who told me to get over it, remember?"

He sighed. "Apparently I'm not as good at handling my own problems. I thought it would be easier if I didn't tell you, but it all got so complicated. And then when I finally *did* tell you . . ."

He let the sentence trail off, right at the part she felt worst about. She took a breath for courage and then finished the sentence for him. "When you finally *did* tell me, I ran out on you. I'm really sorry for that, Danny. It turned out to be so much more serious than

I ever imagined, and I guess for a little while *I* didn't want to have to think about it, either. But I shouldn't have taken off like that—that's not how it's supposed to work."

He looked puzzled. "How what's supposed to work?"

"You know—friendship."

Then she thought of Zandra's family again, coping with R.J.'s autism. They didn't just love him when he was sweet and charming—they loved him during the challenging times, too. And she thought of her mother, who refused to let Anna Mei's thoughtlessness or her own hurt feelings come between them.

"And families too, really," she said. "I mean, it's not okay to be there during the fun and happy times, and then try to escape the hard ones. You have to be there for those, too. It's a whole package deal."

For a minute or two Danny didn't say anything, and Anna Mei worried that he might not accept her apology. But when he did answer, it was more about him than her.

"I see what you mean," he said. "My family had some really great times before all this happened. And Connor was there when I needed him most. I guess I just need to stop being mad that this happened, and that things had to change. It's not my family's fault, after all. I think they're doing the best they can, really."

"I think most families do," she said. "And it

seems like working on their problems together is how they get through them. Besides, your mom really is better, Danny. Even though you were worried last fall, it turned out okay—you're going to have a lot more great times together."

They both looked up as a group of day camp kids hiked along the path, on their way to the education building. A woman pushing a toddler in a stroller walked by, stopping to look for turtles in the pond.

Finally Danny said, "The thing is, I have another big problem I haven't even told you about yet."

Anna Mei's throat felt suddenly dry. She wondered how much more there could be, and whether there'd be anything she could do to help. But whatever the problem was, she would stay and listen, and let Danny know that she was here for him.

"Is this about your mom, too?" she asked.

"Yes," he said, the look on his face matching his serious tone. "The thing is, she's been bugging me for months about meeting you. I didn't want her to see you earlier because I was sure she'd invite you in, so I sort of . . . panicked, I guess. I mean, you didn't know, and she didn't know you didn't know."

Anna Mei tried to follow the logic of this. "Okay," she said slowly. "But now . . . ?"

"Now I'm afraid that if you don't come back to my house with me, she might not let me in the door. And that's a problem because we're having lasagna for dinner."

Then he smiled—the first real, honest-to-goodness Danny Gallagher grin she'd seen in a long time. And she could have sworn that right at that exact moment, the sun broke through the clouds, just like in the movies. How corny was that?

Chapter Thirty-One

A Familiar Ring

The End-of-Summer Backyard Bash had started as a simple idea of Zandra's. She'd wanted to have Anna Mei, Danny, and Luis over before school started again, maybe get some pizza, and play some volleyball.

Once her parents got involved, though, the little get-together to celebrate the end of summer mushroomed into a super-sized party involving all four families.

Now Luis's dad stood at the grill with Zandra's dad, turning out enough burgers and hot dogs to rival a fast-food restaurant. In the kitchen, Mrs. Caine was slicing watermelon while Mrs. Hernandez made more lemonade. The big table practically groaned under the weight of all the food everyone had brought to share.

Anna Mei's mother sat with Danny's mother under the shade of the patio umbrella, chatting away as they watched the two youngest Hernandez girls splashing in the plastic wading pool. Mrs. Gallagher, though a little on the thin side, was nothing like the pale, sickly woman Anna Mei had imagined. Her smile was friendly and warm, and she had the same sparkling blue eyes and Irish charm as her youngest son.

In the driveway out front, Danny's father was playing Anna Mei's father in a game of H-O-R-S-E. Though a good six inches shorter, Mr. Gallagher had issued the challenge, pointing out that accuracy was more important than height in this particular basketball game. It turned out that he was about as accurate as he was tall, but Anna Mei had never seen anyone have more fun losing.

Aleesha, R.J., Marcus, and the oldest of Luis's sisters—Elena—were all keeping score, shouting out the letters in the word "horse" each time one of the men missed a shot. After that all the kids joined in. When Marcus complained that the basket was too high for him, Mr. Anderson hoisted him onto his shoulders, and soon he was making more shots than anyone.

Connor was the only sibling who hadn't come to the party. He'd taken a job doing lawn work for a local landscaping company and Saturdays were an especially busy time. But Danny was taking it pretty well.

"We've been hanging out more lately, ever since I told him I wanted to," he told Anna Mei. "He even took me to see a movie last week. Of course, he made me buy my own popcorn," he'd added, grinning.

"Well, yeah, who could blame the guy for not wanting to go bankrupt?" she pointed out.

Zandra and Anna Mei turned out to be the only ones interested in the volleyball net they'd set up in the backyard. They practically had to drag Danny and Luis over to play a game. Things perked up when Danny suggested that they throw out the real rules. After that it became a hilarious free-for-all of tossing, bouncing, and even kicking the ball. Finally Luis scored the winning point by heading it over the net, as if it were a soccer ball.

They flopped down in the shade after that, gulping lemonade and talking about how quickly the summer had gone by.

"I don't know about you," Zandra said, "but I can't wait for school to start. I'm so excited about going to Westside, after all those years at Elmwood."

Luis shook his head. "I'm not sure 'excited' and 'school' belong in the same sentence, Zandra. Personally I wouldn't say no to another month or two of summer first."

"And I'm kind of going to miss Elmwood," Danny said. "At least we knew what to expect there. It's going to be hard getting used to all new teachers and everything."

"Uh, excuse me," Anna Mei said, poking him with her elbow, "but *some* of us have already managed to conquer that particular challenge. Are you saying you can't handle it?"

"Fine, you're the expert," he said. "If any of us has a problem we'll just call on Cartoon Girl—our own seventh-grade superhero."

"To the rescue!" Luis added, laughing.

"Anna Mei and I will be busy with volleyball," Zandra said. "But I also want to join the swim club. How about you guys?"

"I really liked working on the yearbook," Anna Mei said. "And if there's a science club, I'll be all over that."

"Like mold on month-old bread," Danny said, grinning. "I don't have a club or a sport picked out yet, but I can tell you for sure what it *won't* be."

There was a moment's pause, then all three of the others came up with it at the same time: "Bowling!" they said, and everyone laughed.

"Wait a minute," Anna Mei said, "I left something in the car and I want to go get it. I'll be right back."

When she returned she was carrying her moon and stars notebook, the one that still held all her plans and notes from her first summer here.

"You've got to be kidding," Danny said. "We

haven't even started seventh grade yet and you're already trying to organize it."

"Well, there's obviously going to be a lot for us to do," she said, smiling. "We'll definitely need a list."

The conversation had a familiar ring to it. It reminded Anna Mei of the one they'd had in the Elmwood Elementary cafeteria, when they were all looking forward to summer. Now they were looking forward to starting seventh grade together.

She remembered a time when she was afraid she would never have this feeling again—a feeling that she belonged. But the four of them already shared a history together, and now they would share a future, too. She was pretty sure that whatever happened next, Danny and Zandra and Luis would face it with her. And from now on, she would be a friend they could count on, no matter what. After all, what were superheroes for?

Carol A. Grund first introduced the character of Anna Mei Anderson in *Anna Mei, Cartoon Girl* (Pauline Books & Media, 2010). The enthusiastic response to that story inspired the further adventures of Anna Mei and her friends for this sequel, as well as for the third book in the series, also planned for release in 2011. Carol's stories and poems have appeared in children's magazines and book anthologies, including *Ladybug, Ladybug* (Carus Publishing), *Friend 2 Friend, Celebrate the Season* and *Family Matters* (all from Pauline Books & Media). She has also contributed to several *Chicken Soup for the Soul* collections. Find more about Carol—and a special *Anna Mei* site—at CarolAGrund.com.

Anna Mei

Blessing in Disguise

Coming soon!

You've read all about Anna Mei's move from Boston to Michigan in *Anna Mei, Cartoon Girl*. And you've just finished learning Danny's secret in *Anna Mei, Escape Artist*.

Now get a sneak preview of *Anna Mei , Blessing in Disguise*, and meet someone who will change Anna Mei's life forever....

Chapter 1

Werewolf at the Door

When the werewolf appeared at her bedroom door, Anna Mei Anderson was sitting in her green-striped chair, just starting some math homework. In a horror movie, the situation would have called for some terrified screaming, maybe even a daring escape out the second-story window.

In real life, Anna Mei just shook her head, smiling.

"Hi Dad," she said. "Been going through the Halloween box again?"

Snapping and snarling, he came in and looked at himself in her mirror. "I've already worn all of those," he said, his voice muffled behind all the fake fur and latex. "I wanted something new this year, so I stopped at the costume shop on my way home. What do you think?"

"I think I agree with Mom—when it comes to Halloween, some people never grow up."

Her father peeled off the mask, making his hair stand practically straight up. Lately Anna Mei had started to notice strands of silver mixed in with the blond. Even though she knew he turned forty-six on his last birthday, it seemed weird to think of her father as getting older. To her he always looked the same—tall and thin, with a dent on his nose where his dark-rimmed glasses sat, and a crooked smile that reached all the way up to his blue eyes.

Now he patted his hair down and put his glasses back on. When he turned away from the mirror, he looked like the mild-mannered research scientist that he actually was.

"When it comes to Halloween," he said, "I think *everyone* should get to be a kid. Which brings me to my next question—what about you? Have you decided on a costume yet?"

"Honestly, Dad, I've been so busy since school started," she told him, "I haven't had time to think about it."

"Lots of homework this year, huh?" he asked, looking at the big pile of textbooks she'd dumped onto the bed.

"Well, yeah," she answered, "but that's only part of it. I also have volleyball almost every day, and Science Club every week, plus hanging out with my friends. It all takes time."

"I noticed," he said. "If you get any busier, your mom and I are going to start renting out your room. *Someone* might as well be using it."

"Okay, I don't think it's quite that—*oof!*"

Her cat, who had scooted under the bed when the snarling werewolf appeared, picked that moment to launch herself into Anna Mei's lap, knocking her math book to the floor.

"Have you been listening, Cleo?" Anna Mei said, ruffling the cat's grey and white fur. "I have a feeling you don't like the idea of someone else taking over my room."

Her father reached down to retrieve the book. "Either that or she's courageously trying to save you from death by algebra," he suggested.

As he added that book to the pile on her bed, another one caught his attention. "Wow, this one's huge!" he said, picking it up and hefting it. "It must weigh at least five pounds."

"Tell me about it," she said. "That's social studies. And Mr. Crandall gives homework almost every night."

"*Studies in Culture: Africa, Asia, and Australia,*" Dad read aloud from the cover. "That sounds interesting."

Anna Mei had learned a long time ago that *interesting* often meant something completely different to adults than it did to her. "I guess," she said, shrugging.

"I always wished your mom and I could have seen more of China when we were there," he said, looking through the book for the Asian section. "It's so big—we barely had time to scratch the surface."

Twelve years ago, Anna Mei had been born in Hunan, a province in southern China. She didn't remember it, of course—she had been only six months old when the Andersons adopted her from the orphanage and brought her home with them to Boston. Growing up there, she had rarely given any thought to the fact that her life began somewhere else.

That is, until a year ago, when the three of them moved to Michigan. Suddenly she seemed to stick out like a sore thumb—the new girl who was Chinese and, oh by the way, her parents weren't.

At first she worked pretty hard to prove that she was just like everyone else. But when her sixth grade social studies teacher assigned a class project on heritage, Anna Mei decided to go ahead and tell the class about her birth country. She did some research about the city of Yiyang, where the orphanage was. And she showed them the note her birth mother had pinned to her baby clothes, calling her "Mei Li"—beautiful plum blossom.

After that, she was relieved when no one treated her any differently than before. It turned out that where you were born or what your family looked like wasn't a big deal to most people. But now her father, looking at a map of Asia in her social studies book, seemed to expect her to be excited about studying China, a place almost as foreign to her as Africa or Australia.

"Well, you'll have to get back to me when you get to that section," he said. "Assuming you can find a few minutes to spare for your old dad."

"Hey, it's not like I'm the only busy one around here," she pointed out. "You've been working late almost every night, even on Mom's nights at the hospital. Zandra's parents are the ones bringing me home from volleyball."

"You've got a point there," he admitted. "This project I'm working on is pretty intense. The good news is that the university has promised to hire a consultant, so I'll be getting some help soon."

"It's about time," she said, and knew it sounded grumpy. But she was still ticked off that his project was the reason the family never got to take a trip to Boston over the summer. She had been looking forward to seeing her old friends again, especially Lauren, and going to the places where they used to hang out. That trip had been postponed until her father could manage to get away from the lab.

"Speaking of time," he said, putting the book back down on the bed, "it's getting late. There's either a real werewolf hiding in here somewhere, or my stomach is growling for dinner. How does spaghetti sound?"

"Like this," she told him, sucking in her cheeks and slurping loudly.

He laughed, as she knew he would. The cornier the joke, the more he liked it.

"Okay, give me about twenty minutes," he said, heading out the door. Then he stopped and stuck his head back in. "And start thinking about a costume. Only two weeks left, you know."

She had to smile. It was like he still thought of her as a little kid, getting all excited about going trick-or-treating on Halloween. She would be thirteen in January—he was going to have to notice her growing up sooner or later.

"I will," she promised, then moved a protesting Cleo off her lap so she could get back to her math homework.

Chapter 2

Fifth Period Lunch

A week later, Anna Mei stood at her locker, trying to hurry as she twisted the dial on her combination lock. Her lunch period was starting, and she wanted to spend as much of it as possible with her friends.

Westside Junior High combined all the seventh and eighth graders from the three elementary schools in town, totaling about 400 students. It was smaller than the middle school Anna Mei would have gone to in Boston, but she still thought of it as a step up. She liked being in a place where everyone was around her age. She liked changing classes every fifty minutes, rotating through the school, and having a different teacher for each subject. And given the number of books she was expected to lug around, she liked having a locker to stash them in.

Because lockers were assigned alphabetically, hers was locker number three, right between Martin Alvarez and Maddie Armstrong. Neither of them was here at the moment—they both had fourth period lunch. Anna Mei had that one, too, on Mondays, Wednesdays, and Fridays. But on Tuesdays and Thursdays she had an elective class in the morning that bumped her lunch to fifth period.

Thank goodness for Spanish class, she thought, shoving her books into her locker and grabbing her lunch bag.

Not that it was her favorite class—not even close—but taking Spanish twice a week meant she could have lunch with all three of her best friends. So far, that was the biggest drawback to life at Westside. After being in the same sixth-grade class at Elmwood Elementary, and then hanging out over the summer, the four of them had been excited about going to junior high together. And although they shared a few of the same classes, Anna Mei missed being able to see them all day long.

At least she and Zandra had matching lunch periods every day. On the days Anna Mei was in Spanish class, Zandra had choir. And since her last name was Caine, her locker was just down the hall from Anna Mei's. The two girls headed for the cafeteria together, where today they found Danny Gallagher and Luis Hernandez already at their usual table.

Luis looked up and saw them coming. "*Hola, mis*

amigas," he said. As they sat down, he turned to Anna Mei with a smile. "*¿Y cómo estás hoy?*"

He had grown up speaking Spanish, and now that Anna Mei was studying it, he liked to use it on her. Luckily, "*cómo estás*" was an easy one.

"*Muy bien,*" she answered. "I'm fine. *Gracias.*"

"That's *muy* impressive," Danny told them both. "But for the sake of the non-Spanish speakers sitting here, would you mind switching to English?"

"Okay," Luis agreed, grinning. "As long as *you* promise not to pull out the old 'sure and begorrah' stuff."

Danny looked as Irish as he was, with a wide smile to go with his red hair and freckles. Over the summer he'd gotten taller, Anna Mei noticed. And he was planning to join the swim team next semester, so he'd started exercising more and eating healthier. He still pretty much inhaled his lunch, but at least now it had more fruits and vegetables in it.

Zandra laughed as she took a sandwich and banana out of her lunch bag. "I'd be nice to them if I were you, Danny," she said. "Aren't you taking Spanish next semester?"

"Oh yeah," he said, polishing an apple on his shirt sleeve. "What I meant to say was, feel free to practice all the Spanish you want, *por favor.*"

"Not today, though," Anna Mei said. "We don't have much time, and I don't even know the Spanish word for what I want to talk about."

"Which is—?" Zandra prompted, pulling the lid off her yogurt container.

"Halloween," Anna Mei said. "It's coming up on Sunday, so we need to start making our plans now."

Danny groaned as he picked up his milk carton. "There she goes again, planning everything to within an inch of its life."

"Well, Danny," she said, with a deep sigh, "feel free to wait until five o'clock on Halloween night to decide what you want to do. There might still be time to draw a face on a paper bag and wear it over your head."

She figured he would have some kind of sarcastic comeback, but it was Luis who spoke first.

"Something tells me it wouldn't be the first time," he said.

In the next moment they were all laughing—including Danny. And luckily for the rest of them, he managed to swallow his mouthful of milk first.

JClub
A Catholic Place for Kids

Who are the Daughters of St. Paul?

Pauline Kids

We are Catholic sisters. Our mission is to be like Saint Paul and tell everyone about Jesus! There are so many ways for people to communicate with each other. We want to use all of them so everyone will know how much God loves us. We do this by printing books (you're holding one!), making radio shows, singing, helping people at our bookstores, using the Internet, and in many other ways.

Visit our Web site at www.pauline.org

The Daughters of St. Paul operate book and media centers at the following addresses. Visit, call or write the one nearest you today, or find us on the World Wide Web, www.pauline.org

CALIFORNIA
3908 Sepulveda Blvd, Culver City, CA 90230 — 310-397-8676
935 Brewster Avenue, Redwood City, CA 94063 — 650-369-4230
5945 Balboa Avenue, San Diego, CA 92111 — 858-565-9181

FLORIDA
145 S.W. 107th Avenue, Miami, FL 33174 — 305-559-6715

HAWAII
1143 Bishop Street, Honolulu, HI 96813 — 808-521-2731
Neighbor Islands call: — 866-521-2731

ILLINOIS
172 North Michigan Avenue, Chicago, IL 60601 — 312-346-4228

LOUISIANA
4403 Veterans Memorial Blvd, Metairie, LA 70006 — 504-887-7631

MASSACHUSETTS
885 Providence Hwy, Dedham, MA 02026 — 781-326-5385

MISSOURI
9804 Watson Road, St. Louis, MO 63126 — 314-965-3512

NEW JERSEY
561 U.S. Route 1, Wick Plaza, Edison, NJ 08817 — 732-572-1200

NEW YORK
64 West 38th Street, New York, NY 10018 — 212-754-1110

PENNSYLVANIA
Philadelphia—relocating — 215-969-5068

SOUTH CAROLINA
243 King Street, Charleston, SC 29401 — 843-577-0175

VIRGINIA
1025 King Street, Alexandria, VA 22314 — 703-549-3806

CANADA
3022 Dufferin Street, Toronto, ON M6B 3T5 — 416-781-9131